HOW TO
ACCOMMODATE
MEN

STORIES BY

MARILYN KRYSL

COFFEE HOUSE PRESS MINNEAPOLIS

AUTHOR ACKNOWLEDGEMENT Grateful acknowledgement is made to The Corporation of Yaddo, The Colorado Council on the Arts and Humanities, and the University of Colorado's Council on Research and Creative Work and the Graduate Committee on the Arts and Humanities.

Some of these stories first appeared in the following periodicals: "How To Accommodate Men" in *Blue Mesa* and the anthology *Lovers;* "Laissez-Faire" in *North American Review;* "Extinct Species" in *Glimmertrain;* "Distant Lights on Water" in *Iowa Review;* "The Girls of Fortress America" in *Manoa;* "Glamourpuss" in *Millennium Watch Anthology;* "Mine" in *New American Writing;* "Iron Shard" in *Notre Dame Review;* "In the Upper Reaches, Isis" in *Sniper Logic.* "Mercy" won *Negative Capability's* Award for Fiction, 1994.

Coffee House Press is supported in part by a grant provided by the Minnesota State Arts Board, through an appropriation by the Minnesota State Legislature, and in part by a grant from the National Endowment for the Arts. Significant support has also been provided by The McKnight Foundation; Lannan Foundation; Target Stores, Dayton's, and Mervyn's by the Dayton Hudson Foundation; General Mills Foundation; St. Paul Companies; Butler Family Foundation; Honeywell Foundation; Star Tribune Foundation; James R. Thorpe Foundation; Dain Bosworth Foundation; Pentair, Inc.; the Helen L. Kuehn Fund of The Minneapolis Foundation; the law firm of Schwegman, Lundberg, Woessner & Kluth, P.A.; and many individual donors. To you and our many readers across the country, we send our thanks for your continuing support.

Coffee House Press books are available to the trade through our primary distributor, Consortium Book Sales & Distribution, 1045 Westgate Drive, Saint Paul, MN 55114. For personal orders, catalogs, or other information, write to: Coffee House Press, 27 N. 4th Street, Suite 400, Minneapolis, MN 55401.

LIBRARY OF CONGRESS CIP INFORMATION
Krysl, Marilyn, 1942 –
    How to accommodate men : stories / by Marilyn Krysl
        p.   cm.
    ISBN 1-56689-076-4 (ALK PAPER)
    1. Man-woman relationships—Fiction.   2. Interpersonal relations—
Fiction.   I. Title.
PS3561.R88H65   1998
813'.54—dc21   98-21158
                                                      CIP

10   9   8   7   6   5   4   3   2   1

contents

for the women and the men who teach me, forgive me, love me,
help me understand.

GLAMOUR-
PUSS

1

LAISSEZ-FAIRE

Frank holds a tie in each hand. One is salmon, the other a pattern of green and gold diamonds. His shirt is red.

"Which one?" he asks.

Either is going to be a disaster with that shirt, but I don't say this. It would prick his balloon, and I don't want to play Scrooge, not at Christmas. On the other hand, he wants to make a good impression. I want him to make a good impression. What we do reflects on each other, and now it's these damn ties. I'll note the way people look at him, then at me, sizing me up. Is she the sort who insists her partner meet minimum standards of presentability, or does she discreetly defer?

"How about your blue striped one," I say. You can always improve your product. Frank nods and goes out humming. When he comes back, he's wearing the blue stripe. He's just turned sixty, and his sex appeal is going great guns. The frown lines on his forehead are signs of worldliness. And he's still got a powerful walk. He strides out as though he's just signed a multimillion-dollar contract. He's good for another decade of flirting and looking prosperous.

"I've been looking forward to us going to this together," he says now.

"We always go to your office party together," I say.

"I mean it will be nice to be at the party with *you*, sweet-heart."

There was a time when he stayed by me at parties, showing me off. Now he heads immediately for the bar, gets into conversation. I don't think he's conscious of the change, and why should he be? His stock is going up. It's mine that's coming down. We'll go to this party, and he'll be the man he is, with his classy assets—snazzy vehicle, fourteen-carat credentials, success in the upper echelons of civil service, an attractive wife. His cache depends on others wanting what he's got, and he knows how to manipulate the market. Take my attractiveness. Its value for him depends on that staple of advertising, illusion. I seem in excellent shape for my age. And I agree to work the illusion. I spruce up my inventory, that intangible "presence," something you can't buy (though money helps you cobble it together), which is why its value has shot up. I seem on top of the game, whatever game's going, and Frank gets some of the return.

"We're a handsome couple," Frank says. He kisses me on the cheek. He's affectionate, and not stingy like so many men whose wives have that bargain basement look. Also, I've trained him to pitch in with housework. We have a schedule for who cooks when. You do this, I'll do that. If we don't agree, we negotiate until we do. It's as though we're in international shipping—sailing a ton of cargo here, whipping another two tons off to over there.

Now he holds my coat as though it's a joint contract. He's signed. Now it's my turn.

I chat with Frank's superior, his wife, and three other men I haven't met before. One of them questions the advisability of extending most favored nation status to China. Then we're on to Sarajevo, Rwanda, East Timor and back to the aftermath of the L.A. riots. The wife deplores the latest murder by street gangs. All of us join her in this deploring. Snatches of a conversation behind me waft over. "Not liposuction," someone says. "It's her face. She got an eye-lift." Now one of the liposuction men hails the new sensation in performance art—a woman whose assistants paint her with human blood in front of a scrim featuring coverage of the war in Bosnia. Anxious refugees in Mostar get upstaged by nipples and an arresting triangle of pubic hair.

I'm wearing a chic, crushed velvet sheath, the diamond earrings Frank gave me for our anniversary. On the downside, my neck has started to sag. I used to think of this part of me as my throat, and an asset. It came to the fore whenever I threw back my head, and I threw back my head a lot then, flinging my long hair aside and striding on. Now this part of my anatomy resembles the national debt. Nor do I think of it as my throat. It's my neck. There is nothing romantic about it.

Strolling through the park last week I sat down to watch the kids on swings. A little girl tumbled off and skinned her knee in the sand. She came crying to where I sat beside her mother. The mother looked all of sixteen. She took the little girl on her lap. When her tears subsided, she wanted down again. She looked at me then, and I smiled. I could see her marshalling up her courage to come closer.

"Go on, sweetie," her mother said. "Go see granny."

This remark came at me like a sudden blow to the head. The word conjures a figure who can't cross a street by herself, a person who is unaware that the Soviet Union has collapsed. My soul plummeted. Later I stood before the full-length mirror and gave myself a critical appraisal. There are creases at the corners of my eyes, but I'm still trim, with a nice pair of breasts which don't droop noticeably, and I'm vigorous and full of energy. But value is relative. I look great, when I'm the only one there.

That night I dreamed that a liver spot on my hand had grown large, darkened and risen like a mole. I was horrified, but then circumstances inexplicably changed. Suddenly I was delighted: these great, dark growths were now considered beauty marks. Women were dying to have them. Others faked them, but mine was real.

"The question is," the woman next to me says, "if you dye your hair, should you also dye your snatch?" The canapés are very good, and we're picking and choosing. Across the room three young women have engaged Frank in conversation. He holds forth, they hover attentively. He tells a joke, they giggle. Their breasts have an attractive buoyancy. He gestures extravagantly. The four resemble an ad for Old Spice: *no sweat.*

"When I was in my twenties," the woman says, "for my boyfriend for Valentine's day, I had mine shaved in the shape of a heart and dyed red."

I used to be that brazen, but less conscious of fashion. I was given to flinging my panties right and left as I made my way through life. I did a lot of comparison shopping, trying out samples, looking for the perfect product. But I wouldn't have dyed my pubic hair for anyone.

I try the lentil-walnut paté and consider. I'd pretty much given up those fleshy black-market pursuits for long Saturday afternoons reading in the sun, but now I wonder:

should I still be losing sleep over a projected assignation? Are there no other statements to be made than those written in innuendo and piercing glances?

It used to be that when I walked into a room the air spruced up. I carried an electric charge. Young men found me fascinating. They congregated, offering me hors d'oeuvres, making appointments for coffee the following day. I was Helen without the bad rep, and with a charge account that wouldn't come due. I launched some ships, threatened some perfectly durable marriages. It was all very dramatic, and galvanizing and I gloried in The Eternal Feminine. I could choose or discard, approve or decline, create or destroy.

Now when I walk into a room the air has been spruced up by one of those young girls with spiked hair.

To the young I've become an obligation, like tithing. Young men notice me only at the checkout counter. They want to know if I'd like paper or plastic.

Yesterday as I walked to the corner grocery two young men came up the sidewalk, one in Esprit jeans and sneakers, the other head-to-toe leather, sporting snakeskin boots. Engaged in animated conversation, they didn't look up. I kept to my side of the concrete. Still, at the moment we passed, I collided with the young man in leather. "Oh!" I said. He didn't look at me, deeply invested as he was in discourse, praising the musical virtues of a group called Penis Envy. At the same time, with the studied casualness that comes from assumptions buried so deeply their origins can't be traced, he straightened his arm and used it to move me gently but firmly aside, onto the grass.

I had the distinct feeling something had been stolen from me. But my purse was still slung from my shoulder. I thought of the Haitian soldier interviewed just after the execution-style murder of the minister of justice. "You have seen nothing," he said to the reporter, "so nothing is going on."

The party's crowded now. Conversations take place at high volume. A woman spills champagne down the front of her red-sequined dress. People flirt, people gossip. I step out onto the patio. Frank leans against the banister. Now there is only one young woman beside him, a Barbie doll with cleavage and ringlet tresses the color of black quartz. She suggests the woman in the Lord and Taylor perfume ad: *Zino, the fragrance of desire.*

"Sweetheart!" Frank calls, waving me over. I approach with the distinct feeling I'm trespassing on staked-out territory. Frank introduces me to Barbie. By way of filling her in, he praises my latest promotion, mentions an award I received, and my hefty Christmas bonus. He's proud of my achievement, but it might as well be his: she can't take her eyes off him. He's Ulysses just washed up on the beach, an investment opportunity, a whole new market for her product. She will take him to her father, the king, get the slaves to whip up a banquet.

Suddenly I wish I'd divorced at forty. These things would be easier if I weren't married. I wouldn't have to watch groupies launch themselves at Daddy. I could waltz in and out of parties as I pleased, and there would be no sticky situations. My thought flips back to this morning's paper. In the Most-Admired Competition, Oprah and Queen Elizabeth were tied with a faltering two percent.

I want to like young women like Barbie, but it's not easy. I don't want to lie awake nights imagining Frank starting his second family. If it came to that, the fact that I'd be available would be worthless in this market. Besides, when Frank noticed my stock, I in turn invested heavily. I trained him by walking him through the exercises, giving him lots of chances to get it. He was an eager but slow learner, and I put in my time. A lot of fine-tuning went into the final package. If you lose after all that, you kick yourself. You should have put the money into land.

Frank introduces the topic of extending most favored nation status to China. He and I discuss this. Barbie continues her subliminal assault. Finally I step closer, putting myself smack in the middle of her crosshairs.

"What's *your* take on this?" I say, directing my comment to her, giving her the opportunity for eye contact. "Should we give the Chinese the benefit of the doubt?"

But she manages to smile over my shoulder. Her signals signal her eagerness to put herself entirely at Frank's disposal.

I think of the Empress of Japan, who, at a state function, collapsed in a faint and became mute.

Now Frank takes my elbow.

"I need to speak to Jack before we leave," he says. "Let's go in."

Barbie leans forward, touches his arm.

"Promise me you'll come to my party," she says. "You've *got* to promise me."

It's March, and there are crocuses blooming, new spring in people's steps. I lunch with a friend—poached salmon and the season's first asparagus. Before the check comes, I head for the ladies' room, run a comb through my hair. Suddenly a young woman sweeps in, goes straight for the mirror. It's Barbie. Though my reflection is there beside hers, she shows no sign of remembering she's seen me before. She concentrates on a quality check of the product, gets busy repairing her nicks.

My mother was wrong when she insisted cheerily, as she almost always did, that there was more than enough for everybody. She would not admit the truth: for women there is a shortage. But the market thrives on shortages. Shortages are only a debit if you're the one caught short.

This girl is gorgeous, but she doesn't quite believe it. She imagines flaws because she's been trained to look for them. At twenty I was the product of conflicting reports. I'd been told that I interrupted too much, and that I didn't stand up for myself. That I was too eager, and at the same time too withdrawn. Too pushy, and too shy. Too loud, too soft, too indiscreet, too reticent, too fat, too thin. Too young for what I needed, too old to be so needy.

The result was I felt I'd had only crumbs, the skimpiest, most threadbare of loves. A little hug now and then from my busy mother, prescriptions for moral improvement from dad. I looked sumptuous, but inside I was a starveling, a little match girl hoarding my handful of flares, striking one only when I was desperate.

I needed a shower of gold. And I'd been programmed to believe I was helpless, that men were the ones who would supply what I needed, that sex was where I would at last be fed. I was ravenous, and I went out and shoved my pretty tits in the face of the first man who looked at me longer than he should have. I didn't care whether he had children, a wife, a dying mother. If there were older women around, I swear I couldn't see them. I gave myself to him like I was the Academy Award.

I see this same desperation of juice and cell and soul in Barbie. Nothing seduces like desperation. Men mistake need for passion, and congratulate themselves. They've found a frothy honey pot to stick their tongues into, other guys should be so lucky. You see it in porn films: women crazy for attention, the men reading this as admiration.

Underneath the garter belts and boots with cleats, these girls are the Somalia of the emotions. They crawl across the desert on their hands and knees toward the next polluted spring, dragging themselves on for a handful of mealies.

But the fact is that if there's a drought, nothing grows. Suddenly I want Barbie to feel confident, lavished with strokes and praises. I want to make contact, find common ground. It's ridiculous that we should exist, just now, in opposition. I want to feel some little thread of understanding between us, at least the recognition that we're in this together. Because we are: a day will come when she's going to arrive where I am, and the world in which this happens will not have changed much.

"You've got gorgeous hair," I tell her. We're given to extremes, those of us who've suffered deprivation. We excel in extravagant praise, extravagant blame. She recognizes the mode. Possibly I remind her of her mother, another woman who was no doubt given to extremes.

"Really," I say. "You look stunning. Got a boyfriend?"

"Not right now," she says, grimly. There is no envy in her glance, only dread. And why not: she has no resources with which to meet the crisis my reflection represents. There's a photograph of those pine trees they'd planted at Chernobyl just before the disaster. Afterward their needles, which should have grown toward the light, turned away as though stunned. They began to grown downward, toward the black ground.

Now she throws the lip gloss into her purse and heads for the door.

"Wait," I say. "You're beautiful, you really are. You should enjoy it, it's a gift."

She looks at me in disbelief.

"Get real," she says, and walks out.

EXTINCT SPECIES

—Oceans, I said.

I wanted to make things.

—Continents, you replied. We stumbled around in the dark, poking and declaring. The spurs on your cowboy boots made a faint jingling.

—Inland seas, I said, wrapping my silk skirt around me.

—Islands! you countered.

—Springs, lakes, ponds, streams, roaring torrents! Wetlands!

You looked put out. —Copper, zinc, nickel, platinum, molybdenum, iron! you roared.

Were we in competition then? I decided not to reply.

We lay down side by side at the end of the first day.

I woke first. —Dawn! I crowed.

—What? What are you doing?!

—A little light on things, I said. Now that I could see, I admired my seas from all angles. How I liked the little waves glinting in first glimmerings! But you let out a howl.

—Light! you said. —Can't you leave things alone?

—We couldn't see a damn thing, I said. —You want to go whanging around in the dark, bumping into boulders and gneiss?

—I like it dark! you said. —Besides, cataracts and second degree burns! Melanoma!

—Oh for god's sake! I said. —Vitamin D!

—I like black, black nothingness, the void! you cried.

—Here's what we can do, I said. —We'll split it fifty-fifty. Twelve hours for you, twelve hours for me. Though I insist on a moon that wanes and waxes. And we've got to have stars.

On the third day you stood up, faced dawn.

—Santa Cruz cypress, you called out. —The Chilean larch.

—Malheur wire-lettuce, I answered. —Small's milk pea.

—Box elder! you cried. —Banana!

—Lavender, I sang, a low contralto. —Trout lily.

But each time I conceived a new variety, I had the feeling you took it personally.

—Redwoods! you commanded, raising your voice.

—Baby's breath, I crooned.

—The Giant Sequoia! you thundered.

—Coyote thistle, I trilled.

—Banyans! you roared. —Banyans everywhere!

—You're so cute when you get mad, I teased.

—The bristlecone pine, you hissed through clenched teeth.

Still I was optimistic. We seemed a well-matched pair.

—Sea cucumber, I whispered.

It was evening of the third day.

I felt like a new woman.

—Mammals and marsupials, creatures of all kinds!

You sulked and rolled away from me. The bottle of Tanqueray was empty. You hurled it down. It shattered against that outcropping of Elgin marble.

—Don't you want to get up and make things? I asked.

—All this light hurts my eyes! you said.

—Come with me! I said. —It's more fun with you.

But you scowled and sunk back into your hangover. So off I went and made

the Plains wolf

the Clear Lake Minnow

the Apache trout

the Badlands Bighorn

the Hawaiian land snail

the Ivory-Billed woodpecker

the Sea mink

the Passenger pigeon

the Lanaii thrush

Stellar's sea cow

the Eastern elk

the Xerxes Blue Butterfly

and whales. Greenland whales, Right whales, Humpback whales, Sperm whales, Blue whales, Bryde's whales, Tasman whales, Gray whales, Fin whales, Piked whales, Sei whales, Minke whales, Pilot whales, a whole glorious array! I watched them frolic in the bay until the sun hung low. Then I slogged home, weary and ravenous.

—Any of those potato chips left? I said. —What's for dinner?

But you gave me the cold shoulder. You were pretending to watch the sunset, I could tell. It couldn't be sex, I thought. We'd been having plenty of that. And in fact later that night I had the baby.

—Look! I said. I shook you to wake you.

—What's this?

—Our baby! I said. —Isn't he pretty!

—Why didn't you tell me?

—I wanted to surprise you, I said. —Isn't he a pretty surprise?

—Damn it! Why do you always do this?

—Always? I've never had a baby before!

—But you're always doing *something*, aren't you!

You went stomping off into the dark. When you got back you were drunk. You threw yourself down and began to snore. Me, I'd decided I wanted more.

The fifth day dawned. I stretched, yawned, dandled the baby. I hummed a little tune and approved the shape of my ankles. You were already up, sharpening your chain saw.

—Nice day, I said. —Let's get a cup of coffee.

—I brought you these, you said then, flinging down several shipments of elephant-tusk bracelets, stacks of shimmering furs.

—Oh how lovely! I said. —Where did you get these?

—Africa, you said. —Siberia. The North Sea. This is ivory, you said. You were tall and proud.

—Darling, I said, you are sweet to bring me presents!

While you watched, I tried on the furs, strolled back and forth, showing off my finery. Things were on the upswing, I thought, and shook my ass for your benefit.

—I'll be back at dusk, you said, kissed me and left.

The long sweep of the day opened before me, and I brought forth: red and yellow, black and white, all cuter than cute. When I'd fed them and put them down for a nap, I bathed in the stream, ate some papaya. Then I strolled the Great Plains, admiring buffalo, and climbed around in the Rockies looking at boulders. The Bighorns had had babies, and I frolicked with the new lambs. A cloud of Xerxes floated by, and the sky was a vast and piercing blue.

Then I heard your voice, a guttural muttering in the distance. And another sound: the scream of a machine. I scanned the horizon, and there you were, beyond the Sierras. You with your chain saw, taking down the sequoias.

—What's the point? I hollered. —You just got them up!

—They're mine, you snarled. —Shut up!

Day six. Let me admit it: the children had got out of hand. They required speeded-up production of diapers and Nikes. Their popsicle sticks alone used up New Guinea's rain forest, and their Big Macs took down the one in Brazil. In spite of this, I thought of each birth as a triumph for us both, but your mouth tightened like a vice. You started staying late at the lab, inventing new uses for little known metals. On those rare occasions when you came home, you stayed close to the Tanqueray.

Let me also admit that between the diapers and the birthday parties, I'd failed to notice that the water was turning to brine. Now the air was mostly carbon. On the sixth day you excavated the Sahara and built a dam, but the reservoir didn't fill. What had been desert became a great pit, collecting slag, castaway plastic bottles. By this time most of the topsoil had settled on the ocean bottoms. The coastlines were littered with hulks of beached whales. I searched among the carcasses, but I could not find a Blue anywhere. Suddenly it hit me: with the children whining

I'd stopped hearing whale songs, the trill of the cardinal, the voice in the water, the silence of stones. It was as though I'd cut off a hand or an ear. I stood there, the children around me, hungry, asking when would dinner be ready. For the first time in my life I didn't know what to do.

Evening of the sixth day, and where were you?

Fitfully was how I slept. I woke on the seventh day to your cursing. I looked around, saw the tanks and choppers, the missiles in silos, those fleets of Tridents. You had a GNP and a National Debt. You had clout. But how was all this hardware going to help?

—Honey? I said. —This was supposed to be a day of rest. Truce?

I had the vague hope we might form a United Nations.

—Look at all these kids! you yelled. —I can't move without stepping on one!

—They're little copies of us! I thought you'd like that.

—Did you have to have three point five billion? you said. —And that's going to double in the next forty years!

What with the kids whining and those piles of dirty laundry waiting, I was a little frazzled and I lost it.

—Militarism! I accused. —Ecological thuggery!

—Male bashing! you replied. —Pure and simple frigidity!

—On the contrary, I said. —You're jealous of my fecundity!

—Stupidity! you flung back. —Lack of intellectual rigor! Look at this clutter! Your knickknacks and your beeswax! Your embroidery! Your paint-by-number!

—I have never painted by number in my life! I cried.

It was then I glanced sideways, saw the bodies of the lambs, in piles.

—Oh God, I said. —What good will a sacrifice do?

—Sacrifice? you said. —I'll show you sacrifice.

And you pulled Isaac from the sandbox and dangled his little body over the edge.

—He's yours! I said.

—Maybe he is, and maybe he isn't.

—Please, I said. —I'll do anything you say.

—You damn well will, you said. And you let go.

What I wonder now is this: did you really believe the fault lay entirely with me? Or did you acknowledge your part in it, then look down over the edge at the body of our son and think the only thing to do was pick a fight, the kind in which you could put us both out of our misery?

You stood, looking down. Then you turned from the edge, and came at me. I snatched up the babies and ran away. I ran and kept running into the eighth day.

We met in the Galapagos in the Twenty-First Century. You'd gone blind from excess CPD, but you knew I was there and rolled your chair toward me. One hand a hook, legs gone at the knees. You said you couldn't miss dialysis for more than a day. And you'd quit the Tanqueray, you were in recovery.

Me, I'd had skin grafts, chemotherapy, a hysterectomy. And I was in supplemental deprivation therapy. Most of our creatures were gone. I lacked mink and elk, pigeon and sea cow, thrush and trout. I was taking the drugs, but I did not feel well. There is no real replacement for butterfly and snail.

What was there to say? Most of us was gone. I regretted those bracelets I'd accepted and the furs I'd worn. Most of all I regretted my enthusiasm for the thrill of pregnancy. I'd been a glutton for procreation, and I had rested unseeing in that creatrix self-congratulation.

I lay my hand on your shoulder. Around us the oceans continued to dwindle leaving salt flats, and the sky began falling about us in brittle pieces.

    —Sorry! you said then. —Oh sorry! And Love! you cried.

    —Yes, Love, I agreed. —The Blue whale, I replied.

MERCY

Where, where, damn it, is the queen! The little prince's mother, right now, while she can still save him? Is she in the pantry, eating bread and honey? Is she in the master bedroom stripping the king-size bed, staring at the mattress, that white blank, site of the black-and-blue psyche's insomnia? Or has she flown the coop, avoiding the lily pool, the sounds of scuffle near the flagstones, those blackbirds settling in the elms? Or is this woman finally and for once moving quickly, mounting a white charger, sweeping us up, getting us out of here?

But that would show decision, resolution. Conviction. Queenly qualities. Or are these kingly qualities? Is that why she lacks them? Because in a queen they would be unbecoming?

Is that the smell of roast beef or a pie?

And the maid. Is she in the garden hanging out the clothes? But there is no maid, the queen serves as maid, we've done away with slavery, though not its modern counterpart, the service class. They tell her she's a queen, and she does her best to believe this, even when her feet ache from eight hours behind the checkout counter. Does she throw herself into this belief the way the religious do, is this why she has this maddening talent for being absent, because belief in the face of evidence to the contrary takes one's full attention?

What time is it? Time for the queen to come home. How the little prince wishes she would. He plays trucks with the neighbor boy, whose mother baby-sits them after kindergarten. Even if it weren't time he would wish it were, for he believes when his mother's here nothing bad will happen. Though there is little basis for this belief, he clings to it. Simple safety is what he hopes for. A quotidian afternoon in which nothing much happens is a gift. He does not trust extremes—one end of the spectrum is much like the other, both invite overwrought emotion, and even declarations of love delivered with intensity may lead to excruciating disappointment when it turns out the declarer is unable to deliver on these assertions.

He prefers benign neglect, as do I. We don't ask for love, kindness, ease, a little joy—just the absence of atrocity. It would be most good, the little prince imagines, if the king wasn't especially interested in him. And the best guarantee is his mother's presence. Though she fails to protect him, he continues to believe she will.

If only she were in the pantry eating bread and honey! But they give each other room, the king and queen, they have an uncanny way of avoiding witnessing each other's tactics. Even when the queen is present she goes blank, as though a curtain has dropped across her consciousness, or is it a steel door? You can be saved, psychoanalysts say, if there is one other person—only one—who takes issue with the authority figure, and by so doing, demonstrates that another order exists. Our mother would be the logical candidate for this role. But she's an expert at not seeing not hearing not smelling not tasting not feeling the things of this world. Is it because she seems so hopeless that we focus our anxiety on the king?

Now look: someone has let the king's blackbirds out! They've flown the coop, see their black hovering!

Someone will have to pay for that.

It's the era of the two-child family, one of each sex is thought to be ideal, this is an ideal family. I am biding my time, enduring childhood until that moment when I will be able to turn my back on these people and walk out forever. How it shines out there in the future, that silver moment! Meanwhile I make myself scarce and throw my energies into willing my own magical disappearance. I will the king to disappear as well, which works occasionally but only temporarily. If he's not at home, he's on his way home, and even when he leaves for work he'll be back only too soon. Like my brother, I imagine benign neglect, but I am old enough to know it's the exception. There is little domestic uneventfulness here. Intense eventfulness is the rule, and my brother looks like he's disappearing. At age five, you can scarcely see him, scarcely hear his voice. He's in kindergarten and not doing well, but how could he be—already he has his own amazing history to occupy him. He's bright but occupied, the way one country gets occupied by a bigger, smarter, crueler country. He's sick in some way no one talks about, or has been made sick—if we can call it that, torn as we are between illness as an explanation of behavior and the need to affirm individual responsibility in a Sartrian sense—the sick person has a personal responsibility to get well, and not to choose is to choose—though in the case of a five-year-old this seems ludicrous, don't you agree. See how he stills himself, drawn inward, breath held, time suspended—if only it might be suspended indefinitely!

But it's no good. Disaster is imminent, though my mother and father are still at work, and my brother is next door playing at the neighbor's. I lie on my bed, Nancy Drew's adventure open before me, but now I push the book away. Things have become oddly quiet, and quiet is not benign but demonic. It precedes disaster, therefore making disaster inevitable. What time is it?

Back a few weeks, the little prince sitting before a turquoise Melmac plate, set with the usual feast for a king. The little prince himself is a feast for a king, it's Saturn all over again, our father eating meat and forcing others to do the same. What ugly pleasure there must be in this, though the king does not look as though he's enjoying it. Rather he gives the impression of being driven, an invisible knife at his back drives him.

"Eat," the king says. Around us the subdivision replicates itself, a house or two away a voice rends the air, a man's voice yelling, a woman's voice protesting, the man's voice ascending to a rant. I stuff some of the meat in my pocket, make myself swallow the rest, get up and go into the living room in the hope they will forget me because I'm harmless. From my vantage point I watch the queen standing at the sink, scrubbing a pot. Maybe this time she'll tell the king to shove it, lift my brother in her arms, save him from the atrocity of steak cut into bite-sized pieces. But the king admires force, forcing down flesh gives him pleasure. You could say we are force-fed. He believes meat is the essence of manhood, steak and roast beef make a man of you. I hate meat, meat makes my body somnolent, and I do not want to become a man. My brother too, if meat is required, would prefer to forego manhood, but the king requires the mastication of flesh at his table.

The rope is white cotton, the kind the maid would hang the clothes on, if there were a maid. He won't untie my brother until the meat is gone. But we're in luck! Now the king takes a break from the inquisition, throws aside his napkin, goes into the living room. He likes sometimes to stew in his rage alone, to enjoy the familiar feel of it roiling in his belly. He likes to string it out, as he was once strung out by it. Though women's work is never done, the queen finishes the dishes, wipes the counter, rinses and wrings out the sponge. Then she unties the little prince. She makes it seem routine, though routinization increases rather than diminishes the demonic aspect, don't you agree. He clings to her, presses his face against her shoulder. Her body, he thinks, is like music, a place in which he need not fear— but this sanctuary lasts only a few moments.

"Time for bed," she whispers. "Shhh, don't make noise." She carries him upstairs. I know what happens there, she can't hold him forever, she wants him into bed, out of sight, out of mind. Whatever it is that's on her mind is on it relentlessly, and she cannot acknowledge the suffering of others, especially her own children, who seem only to remind her of what she most wants to forget. The little prince might be happy a little longer, he might experience another few moments of bliss, his mother holding him beside the open window, oh good the window frame, lovely the night when a boy is in his mother's arms! But she lays him down. "It's all right," she says then, though of course she lies: it isn't all right now, nor will it be in the future. "Goodnight," she whispers, leaving a wedge of light across the floor.

The little prince tries to bring together in his mind her judgment of the world and his perception of it. As Freud decided to understand his patients' reports of incest in such a way as to keep the adult's virtue intact, so we ache to keep the father, the mother, the teacher noble, or if not noble at least elevated, certainly innocent of malevolent intent. She is his mother and therefore his bright coin, and there is no end to what the imagination can imagine. He works to imagine that what she says is true.

You wonder about this king and queen, and so do the behaviorists, eager to establish how this man and woman got this way. The king himself cannot remember a time when he was not aware of the inevitability of eventually assuming the throne. When a thing is established its force is palpable, and it was in this atmosphere that his sense of primogeniture formed. It was given as gravity, it was always going to be this way, but just in case the charged atmosphere failed to do its work, his parents made sure he got the message. His father locked him in the dungeon, creepy, damp, and no light—never underestimate the power of darkness. He lay there for indeterminate lengths of time. Even now he can't remember whether it was days or merely hours. And his mother did nothing, which is why he's married a woman who resembles her in this crucial aspect. Either his mother agreed dungeoning was for the best, or she was simply too fearful to question the father's decision. Perhaps both. His father locked him up with just enough frequency to keep up the pressure, but not too frequently, because he didn't want the boy to get used to it. The boy understood he was being groomed: his duty and his fate were there like the world was there, like his father was there, fixed and eternal. And when he heard his mother whimpering behind the closed door, he understood he would have to learn this too, making women cower would become his responsibility. He was nothing if not obedient, think of armies in formation, think of those masses in white on their knees, foreheads to the mat. It's the same in Dayton as it is in Weisbaden, anywhere at all you can hoist a flag and get rid of the peasants, rip a woman's teeth out or shave her head, there's power in teeth, in hair. The king understood the parent is right, and he leaned forward, hoping to learn faster, to get the point they wanted him to get.

Ditto the queen, daughter of a slapped around mother and a father given to slapping around. We wonder was there ever a furious queen and weak king, but it scarcely matters, one way or the other they teach the lesson together, it passes down the generations like inheritance. What happens must happen, and the behaviorists have their data now, the furious king and the weak queen whose fathers and mothers were also furious and weak.

I tiptoe into my brother's room and look at his face, the innocent face of a small child sleeping. Innocence fascinates me, because there is so little of it. I want to smooth the peach fuzz of his cheek, to wrap him against me, to offer him the kindness of the body, the tenderness I do not get but which I know exists. I touch his cheek lightly with the backs of my fingers. Now the crucial question: who am I? If I'm someone, why haven't I saved him? But I will, I plan to, when the day comes, I lean toward that future day. In the meantime I'm just another peasant, watching and waiting, another religious fanatic hoping for rescue by angels. I do not act. I fail even to protest. I am guilty, and to witness my brother's pain is my punishment. But to admit I have failed to protect him is to know I have the power to protect him. I have it, but I don't use this power because to use it might be expensive. Thus I flagellate myself, and thus the fantasizing of angels.

Social scientists theorize intervention. Intervention is the only way to break the chain of obedience. I imagine the things she might do. She might call the police. I imagine officers arriving, bringing order and justice to the world, hauling the king off, removing him neatly from our lives. I who know nothing of law enforcement, how the police are after all the king's men, how they have their own investment in the present order of things, how they will suspect her allegations are exaggerated, pat her on the shoulder and leave. Or she might insist the king stop. I imagine her defying him, how her defiance would stop him in his tracks. I am too naive to understand this too would be futile. The king will not stop, or if he does, only for a while. Then he will start again. Still she might step between him and my brother, put her body there in the bright, cruel air! How it might gleam, her female flesh, thrust in the king's way! And afterward? Still she might do it, step into the burning world and stay there, burn. She might even seize the initiative and cook up a little revenge, the king's own blackbirds baked in a pie, oh that would be a dainty dish! I imagine her throwing herself heart and soul into this baking. And while the pie steams in the oven, as the smell of burning feathers begins to seep into the air, she might call up the white charger, mount, lift the prince and me, settle us against her, carry us off to a distant kingdom. She could do this, she has a little money, she must—after all, she works. She could save us if she decided to—in her case existential responsibility seems entirely to the point. She's an adult, and I hold adults responsible.

Instead she cultivates deafness, blindness. She must not see what is unpleasant, or if she forgets and sees, she takes a fatalistic attitude. Such things happen, how could it be otherwise? She knows how kings behave, there are no surprises, and it's best to make the best of things, though making the best of things is just more women's work, which is never done. Plus she has a job, on her feet, a smile on her face, keep it up, keep it lively, don't keep the customer waiting. The key is to suppress thought and keep moving. She'd like to have courage, but where does one get it? They expect you to manufacture something out of nothing, and how can she, in a kingdom without resources. Still we continue to think of it as her problem: she got herself into this, thus she's responsible for getting herself out. Oh ugliness, the failure of courage! She covers it over with nail polish.

What time is it?

Is that the smell of roast beef or some kind of pie?

Why do I fasten on our mother as the only possible savior? Why not our father? He's as likely to change as she is, which isn't likely, but I cannot admit this. I know I am a child and therefore powerless, but I must have hope. Without hope I will not be able to manage the terror of my weakness, and she is the only other adult here. If I am doomed to be like her, and I believe I am, then I want her to rise up and save us, as I myself hope someday to be able to rise up and save myself and my brother. Plus maternal instincts are supposed to sweep over her, transforming her weakness into a sword. Let there be transformation, let there be a sword—

There *is* a sword, the toy sword our father carved from a length of pine for my brother—

But there is no transformation. And there is no explanation, though the Marxist materialists like to try. Money,
they say, is a problem for the queen, always and endlessly.
Funny, she almost never talks about money, though it has
conditioned in large part her responses and thus deter-
mines more than we like to admit her existential decisions.
She has not had the luxury of a substantial and predictable
economic base from which to imagine a life other than the
one she now leads. Her deliberations, piddling, are over
small, inconsequential amounts of money which, however,
taken together, add up. This is a two-income family, and
two incomes could theoretically do it, but there are contin-
gencies which unfortunately necessitate her dependence
on the king.

By the way, what ever happened to beauty? Look at the
house, a tract on the edge of the tract, the obligatory picture window, a few trees at the side of the house, the lawn
green, weeds along the driveway. What's that song, little
boxes made of ticky-tacky, though she too works. She
works and is too weary to protest the absence of beauty,
and to whom, anyway, would she protest? It's all she can do
to get to work, get back, keep up with the dishes, laundry,
cleaning, shopping—there are times, pushing a cart down
an aisle, when she feels if she has to look at another pork
chop she'll puke—and then there isn't enough left to pay
the neighbor.

"What did you do with your check?" the king says. He
frowns, certainly a frown is justified, you would think her
check would cover the baby-sitting and then some, including picking up his suit at the cleaners and buying his cigarettes, all of which taken together constitute an overage,
or is it a shortage, it depends from which perspective you
consider it. Don't get upset, speak calmly, lay out how the

money was spent, how much went for what, tell him what he already knows but pretends not to, because he wants to use this interrogation against her. He wants her to have to explain because it puts her on the defensive, which automatically elevates him to a position in which he can lord it over her. After all, he does manage always to have money left over, at least so he implies, though often he declines to produce this spare cash, so one might well wonder whether he actually has it in his wallet. Money constitutes authority, cash in the pocket can be used as a weapon, and he enjoys this little contretemps in which, by scarcely raising a finger, and because he has her willing cooperation, he manages to make her very uncomfortable.

Smell that roast, ummmm.

The king is in his counting house reluctantly and triumphantly counting out a little cash for the queen.

Not a roast or a pie this time but a cake. Back a few days, the queen buys party favors, colored paper plates, balloons, streamers. She puts together a cake, tendrils of hair damp against her forehead, slips it into the oven. Then it's done, she lets it cool, prepares the frosting. The guests arrive, other mothers and sons, two girls. A birthday, sometimes, is an island in a wide and torturous sea. The king is at work, and the little prince is safe here, he thinks, inside the party. Dainty the little girls, kind the mothers, and the presents glittering, balloons in clusters, the white frosting. And the faces of the boys. Perhaps these boys can be his friends after all, maybe he can go to their houses instead of next door, there *are* safe families, he believes this, if only he can find a way to get to them, if only one of them will like him enough. Friendship is rescue, and if you have it you can hide it under the bed and bring it out again later, shining. His heart speeds up with dangerous hope!

But it's over too quickly. A boy and his mother go, one by one the boys and their mothers go. Oh short happiness, small the hour of safety. One girl stays longer, he watches her face, her shy smile as she examines his new baseball cap. He lifts it and sets it on her head, but he gets it wrong, he is too eager and he hurries, a little desperately. Her face is puzzled, she demurs, there is no time to do it again the right way, and if there were could he call up the right instincts, he who has had no practice in niceties. How he wants another chance! But the party's over, the girl carried off by her mother. He presses against the mesh of the screen door, watching the girl and her mother go off to the street, their car. *Over.* The blade of a guillotine, cutting this moment off from the others.

Disobedience: so high, so beautiful, and so far away we do not imagine we ever will reach it. Mired as we are in fear. I saw it once, long ago, before my brother was born. I saw it, and I went toward it. I myself was shining then, light reaching toward this other shining. My body everywhere put forth light—and then something happened, the thing I can't remember. Now my body is a blank space, a place of emptiness. Something was taken from me, and afterward my body, though slight, took on a leadenness. I was often drowsy then, and did not want to eat. I slept as much as they would let me.

Now I make my body do the things they want. I stifle complaint and eat meat, do what they say and do not do what they say not to, and above all I do not ask questions. It's as though I don't have a body, though I know I do, but

I avoid it, it isn't safe. In the body they can snatch you up without a moment's notice. Only the mind is safe, imagining angels.

Thus I become their example: a good girl, obedient and docile. I seem to feel nothing, especially when they're watching. I am the example they use against him, and in that way I help them hurt him, and I watch and do nothing to stop them. If there are gradations of obedience, I am the most obedient, mesmerized by fear, dumb with fear, a dumb, recording instrument. I sleep and sleep because I'm afraid.

Then I'm awake, and there is the watching and the waiting in between.

Where are the social workers, the Christian do-gooders, or the primary school teacher who suspects and makes it her business to inquire. No one notices my sunken drowsiness, my brother's paralyzing fear, or if they notice, they do nothing. Or perhaps they cannot act, they too have learned the lesson, they lack disobedience, so that the theory of intervention is beside the point because there are no interventionists. And though there are those who will say the state should provide such services, those who say this are well-meaning but naive. The state is the result of primogeniture, the state exists to back the king in his rage, to keep the queen busy and the princes and princesses either trembling or numb. Rats in control boxes, monkeys chained before levers, birds trained to peck the red door in the white frame even when the food has been withdrawn. Lab assistants have watched these birds peck themselves to death. No one comes. Intervention, if it comes, must come from inside us. But we've learned the lesson: who are we to intervene?

I am too young to imagine how the king and queen got this way. Only much later will I be able to say *Give the king a break,* the man works hard, up at dawn and into a suit and anxiety. You have to go into the jungle if you want a diamond, and a man has to do it the boss's way: pick up that shit, you with the grin on your face, and don't assume, I'll tell you when to smile. A man shuts the self and seals it, then prostrates himself, puts his forehead to the mat, comes home beaten. And it's then, come home to his castle, that he decides by god to become a man! Wouldn't you? He wants his beer, he deserves his nookie, he'd damn well better get agreement. A man needs meat on the table, and if it's not there, someone will have to pay for that. There is a price for everything and someone pays it, though the one who pays is not always the one who gets what they pay for. Cut the king some slack, someone back there promised him a rose garden and then failed to deliver, and he's pissed. Wouldn't you be?

Who let those blackbirds out? Son of a bitch! Here they are, swirling around him. Today, the day the messenger arrived—not even on his knees pleading for clemency, but upright and matter of fact—announcing the surprise attack from the West! Completely unexpected, this blow, the kingdom under threat from without. He has just come from giving the messenger audience—and now these damn birds! Who, he asks himself, his blood pressure climbing, has had the temerity to sneak in and slip the lock?

If only there were a maid to distract him, she might unlace her bodice and detain him, he might forget the reason for his rage, indulge himself in her delicious flesh and then, spent, sleep. But this salvation would be temporary. If there were a maid she would be in the king's employ, she would hang out his laundry, feed his blackbirds, do his bidding, and let him have his prerogatives, as many of them as he cared to claim. Things would remain much the same, we know this from the study of history, which we're advised will prevent us from repeating our mistakes, but doesn't. Man is a thinking animal, the measure of all things, a little lower than the angels, but maids consistently fail to dissuade those in power from performing their atrocities. You know what, but you don't know when. You know it's imminent, but what form will it take this time?

Even near death we hunger for the beautiful. The very sick girl wanted to smell lilacs before she died, but there were no lilacs in September. "Bring my daughter," said Louis XII on his deathbed. "I will look on her face." The little prince heard music on the neighbor's phonograph, or was it the radio, high up on a shelf, a chorus singing. Late winter, and the repetition of these sounds transfixed him in pleasure—until his playmate tugged his sleeve, said, "Come on!" The little prince took that chorus for angels. He had heard the angels singing. Later—two days? three?—he asked his playmate's mother to play the record again. But she misunderstood, or got distracted by a pot boiling over, the worry over a bill in the mail, her husband's unexplained absences, the pain, intermittent, in her lower back. Or she knew what he meant but pretended she didn't, deliberately and out of spite keeping from him the one thing she guessed might afford him solace.

The little prince was afraid to ask again. Had it been a biscuit, he would have looked around the kitchen until he found a biscuit, then eaten it in secret. But beauty is not a biscuit. Beauty is wondrous and therefore intimidating, and he had not been sure where the sound had come from.

Since he was afraid to ask again, he hoped instead to remember the music. He tried to bring it into his mind, to memorize his memory of it. In bed in the dark he worked tenderly, embracing memory. He'd only heard the voices once, but he tried to sing them again to himself, though as time passed they became more difficult to remember. After a while the fact of their sound faded and became memory, became later still a generalized ache for music, and even later a diffused but sharp longing for something he could neither remember nor name.

I too hunger for the beautiful. I'm a sucker for the tiniest bit of color, the shape of a petal, the curve of a bowl. Bird song. Those lush pictures of gods and goddesses I find accidentally in a book. Our Father Who Art In Heaven deliver me from ugliness, grant me the luxury of common decency, let me go unharmed amidst the loveliness of this world, and if that cannot be, then deliver me into the bosom of beauty. I worship the tiniest flowers, the tinkling of water dripping from spigot onto stone. These things sustain me when there is no other sustenance, and they are becoming increasingly important as I begin to suffer disillusionment with angels. I do not want to give up on angels, but I am beginning to wonder: if angels come only in dreams, what good are they? I lie here, sensing the advance of disaster, and it occurs to me to ask myself: what good is the imagination if it can't bring forth an angel at will?

Suddenly I'm afraid. Fear is the real hell, not what happens but fear that it will, that it may be going to happen soon, and if not soon then later, but later is worse, better sooner, then fear is shorter. Of course this is only a hope, we have no say in the timing, and isn't that the point, after all, to keep us guessing. In the end it happens without a printed announcement. Children are not allowed to escape the story of the parents, there's Saturn, we've seen Goya's painting. Others put their hands to our fate, others shape our little existence, raise carnivorous blackbirds. Others taste profits, eat whipped cream with a spoon, insist on their way because they can. They pack the board, they get very drunk, get very sober. I do not tell you this because you will learn from it. We do not learn much, and then we forget. Perhaps, in fact, we can learn only once, and what we learn then is that there is one lesson and one lesson only: holy of holies, the parents are absolute.

How will it come, I wonder, closing the book, the end of everything? Note that the situations of oppressed and oppressor resemble each other. Set aside for a moment the extremity of torture. In that case the oppressed is in no position to show mercy. He may, if he lives, forgive the torturer, but at the moment of torture there is no one in his power, thus to whom would he show mercy? Though he can perhaps forgive himself, if he can feel in those moments that he has a self. But later, in situations outside the extremity of torture, different terms apply. The oppressed may lack the wherewithal to prosper but still have power over others, a woman, say, or a child or an animal or a bit of earth planted with seedlings. In this case the oppressed has the option to show mercy. He may choose to obey the lesson or to disobey.

The oppressor may also obey or disobey, and is free to make this decision at any time. He may choose not to disobey, on the suspicion that showing mercy may compromise his status, but the choice remains his, and not to choose is to choose. The kicker is that both oppressed and oppressor have been taught not to consider their options. It's the nature of obedience that things seem immutably fixed. The king has no sense of the fluidity of possibility. Mercy may simply not occur to him, because for him, as for the oppressed, the parent is sacrosanct. Even he who rules his little kingdom with impunity lacks the wherewithal to flip his father the bird.

I imagine a loaded gun, but where would I get one? Poison, but *what* poison, and how would I get them to drink it? This isn't a fairy tale where a few drops of the deadly are undetectable in a glass of nectar. A knife seems feasible, if I did it while they slept, but as soon as I'd stabbed one the other would surely wake and prevent me from finishing the job—my father first then, but would my mother forgive me? I want to kill them, but I don't want to kill them, not really, because then I would be like them. Escape depends on defining myself away from them, as far away as I can get.

Now the king comes home early. It's the queen who usually comes to get the prince, but today the king appears instead.

My brother becomes immediately wary.

"Can I stay and play?" he asks. He is innocent, the toy truck in his hand.

"You come with me," the king says. Sons are supposed to admire their fathers. Why's this kid so slow to get it? He brings his son home, gets a beer from the fridge, stares out at the houses, their replication. Repetition is something he knows. It has a beat: the steady, repetitive beat of a beating. The queen's at work, she hasn't been served notice, a fact that, unbeknownst to her, elevates her suddenly above her husband. So that he thinks *Where is she,* knowing very well where she is, but taking the attitude that she should be here, where he wants her. And now he remembers those blackbirds. Who has had the temerity to spring the cage and let them fly!

When the prince was four the king took the trouble to carve him a toy sword out of wood. Odd, and he has never done anything so personally deliberate again, but that's part of the pattern, isn't it, little events which seem to belie the fact. Exception takes us by surprise—is he then a more complicated figure than we'd thought, as capable, perhaps, of good as of evil. Exception affords my brother and I the experience, however fleeting, of hope. Hope, that drug we shoot up with. Hope, will of course be disappointed.

It strikes the little prince to take the toy sword to the lily pool. He dips its blade in the water, imagining the water is a great stone, see how easily he draws out Excalibur! See how it glistens! He raises it to the light—

I turn over and press my face into the pillow. If only I were a witch, I could disappear. Or terrorize the king, scare him away from us, change our mother into a different woman, resourceful and attentive, a woman I might want to become. The king saunters out, kicks idly at weeds around the pool's lip. Man, proud man, dressed in a little brief authority. Think of Abraham leaning above Isaac, think of the coat hanger down the throat. You tell by a timbre in the voice not there moments before, you feel a tremor in the air, the light and the elements lean close and whisper: *beware*—

"Take off your clothes," the king says. "I'll teach you to swim." He unbuttons the little prince's shirt. Domestic sounds from the neighbors' houses, but neighbors respect each other's privacy, a man's home is his castle, and though the castle is dingy and of cheap stuff, the right to privacy is a divine right. The king takes his time, the seconds in his hands stretch and sag, there is a delicious and tantalizingly held back quality about these seconds, he wants to draw out the moment in order to possess it. Now the little prince stumbles, one foot caught in his pants leg, how unfortunate. He seems clumsy, which he isn't, but the king decides he is. Nakedness looks like helplessness, and isn't this boy's body small, smaller than the king had thought, and pale, the skin so thin he can see the blue veins beneath, and the little legs. The king thinks about beatings, how fine the arm feels again and again slamming down, but he does not allow himself to indulge this. Restraint kicks in now, he kicks it in when it serves the purpose of extending desire. Also restraint is less messy than indulgence, difficult though restraint is, seeing that frail, inviting body.

He lifts his son, swings him over the water. I am in hiding, but the shut door's no preventive, I know when things are going bad. And who am I? Am I someone? Or do I merely take impressions? I feel my father's excitement rising toward me, and my brother's fear. I am a magnet drawing these energies, and I stand up, open the door. Is something burning? Has my mother come home and put something in the oven? I go downstairs. Something is wrong, I smell it, I feel it in my muscles: the ache of apprehension.

The window looks out onto the backyard. My brother stands waist deep in the lily pool. "I can do it," he says. Suddenly he's hopeful. If he can swim it may please his father enough. "I can swim myself."

"No you can't. You're too little. I'll help you."

I see the king reach out, push my brother's head down. Our mother has not come home.

Still, I think, the king might suddenly think of mercy, why not, it would take so little to stop, the mind flicking just one notch over, how easy it might be to disobey. I've imagined this moment, miraculous and sudden, but simple really, the enactment of my angel theory in which human beings act like angels. Mercy, I think, clutching the iron bars of my mind.

My brother's breath gets away from him, his arms flail upward, fingers grab the king's hand. I see the white helplessness of my brother's grasping. Now the king thinks of those blackbirds: ruling a kingdom ought to be easier than it is—they don't tell you the effort it takes to shut the peasants up, how you have to remind the ones too stupid to remember, how you have to repeat and repeat. And now who am I? Am I no one? *I knew, I knew,* it's as though I make it happen because I imagine it will—

I'm a scream, aloft, flying toward them, through the door, across the grass, my mind burning toward my brother's mind filling up with water. I fly, I have become in the moments the beauty of disobedience, I am now this terrible and great shining, I am what the king cannot abide. Now the king hears my scream, sees me flying, wrapped in my filmy, white disobedience, a garment radiant, blinding, with feathers, with wings.

But my brother has stopped thrashing.

Beneath the green filter of water his tiny body is still.

The king stands, heaves my brother onto the grass. I kneel beside him. Our father seems not to have heard my scream, seen my flying. Am I only a gnat then, a thing so small he need not even flick it away? Our father shakes his head, as though my brother and I are hopeless, he's washing his hands of us. He walks toward the elms.

I hold very still, as though holding still might matter, as though if I am very, very good maybe Our Father Who Art

In Heaven will take this back. And now the queen appears, stands on top of the porch steps, looking out. She seems not to notice the king, his breath quick, short breaths as though from exertion. Nor does she notice the blackbirds settled in the elms, winking flashes, black with an obsidian blackness. She is preoccupied with the drudgery her body has become, the prospect of the predictable, dull tasks she must now perform again, repeating them without satisfaction. And don't forget to keep an eye on the clock.

But the clock has stopped.

My brother does not move.

Let us suppose his soul has risen above his body into Paradise. Isn't it better that it's over at age five, his soul in a place where the soft, luminous air surrounds him, the blooming smell of shrubbery, grass, and through the grass a path of smooth stones bordered by trees, each branch a billowing of leaves? I imagine this for him: let there be grass, stones, trees. But the queen speaks.

"Come on Honey, get up. Let's get you a towel."

And my brother hears her voice. His eyes open. The clock is ticking. Even now, almost safe in Paradise, he lacks disobedience.

She calls, and he comes back into his body, raises his head, sits up. Stares out, amazed.

I do not think *I have saved him*. I think *the sweetness of his body*, the dampness of his breath. The warmth of his cheek when he sleeps.

And now, the next moment: the moment in which I understand that my brother and mother are one. It is a moment mediated by that longing for beauty. My brother does not recognize for what it is that which is before him: our ticky-tacky mother, the depressed houses, the shame of the cheap subdivision, yards watered and cut, overgrown with weeds, it's all the same amidst the abandoned by God. Instead he sees the splendor of light in the grass, the obsidian flicker of birds amidst the elm leaves. He sees our mother, source of the world, body of all abundant things.

I am present at this indelible moment, watching: my brother looks at her, and he is happy in mercy, shining in the bestowal of mercy, *he believes she has shown him mercy.* How clearly I see his mind, working: our father's infamy now subsumed and made smaller in my brother's idea of the merciful mother. And my brother's gratefulness at this show of mercy turns the world around him into a splendrous thing. Though this is an illusion, my brother's gratefulness will not be gainsayed. In a boy so small, it will find its object. It will, if need be, manufacture its object. Hear my brother's mind sing! See the mind prostrate with gratefulness: those masses in white rows, foreheads to the mat, the mass voice droning like a human bell.

Hear now the anthem of obedience: *Mother I love you, Father I'm so happy.* My brother will not let go the idea of the shining father, fixed and eternal, standing behind the gleaming mother, the two like statuary, naked and powerful, their world indestructible, world without end. He will do anything for them, he will be dead for them to please them, and he will dedicate the rest of his life to serving those whose faces were the first faces.

And who am I, in this moment? The perceiver, the taker of impressions. I see the grass, my radiant brother. Our mother standing in a shaft of late light looks older than I remembered. Our father, off to the side, stands where grass meets the elms, frowning casually, as though this is an ordinary evening, as though nothing much is going on.

You want me to say that my brother escapes. You want me to say that eventually we both escape. We grow wings, we turn into shining, merciful beings. I keep watch, I note any new evidence. I keep an eye on things, just in case they're about to change. I look, I listen, I feel the air on my skin, sniff this air.

Is that the smell of a pie, or a roast?

IN THE UPPER
REACHES, ISIS

I'm in love with the pollinator.

Far below, near the beach, the racket of explosives. The mercenaries—flack jackets and helmets, brandishing uzis. A landscape of shattered glass, battlements that were once foundations of dwellings. We're too high up to see, but we know what happens. Three of them come upon a fourth. One holds him at gunpoint, while the other two beat him with the butts of their rifles. When he's still, one examines his tags: turns out he's one of their own.

A bride, I step into the white nylon suit, gear that resembles the feathery chiffon of angels. The pollinator kisses the nape of my neck, then takes me by the hand up through the banana trees, their leaves like fans, past the sword leaves of the hala. The more we ascend the less dense flesh feels, our rising part hovering, part flight. Energy, like bubbles in champagne, bright little stings. My arms feel fluttery. We're growing wings.

Somewhere above us, the Ooallecia, gush of amaryllis orange. Blossom with sextet petals. In this heat they fall open by themselves. There are twelve Ooallecias left, and the pollinator knows where they are. He takes the

place of the Divenet, that streak of blue that used to dip
its beak into petaled throats. The Divenet is gone now, and
we who are left have migrated higher each year, away
from the cities and the war. Like the Divenet, we drink
dew and gathered rain. We eat seeds, fruits, tubers, insects
that have become delicacies. Like the Divenet we sleep in
trees.

I was in flight when I met the pollinator at a wind dance on
the limestone plateau. I'd serviced my last soldier. They're
all mercenaries now, in it for the money. Valor doesn't exist,
so how can a woman admire them. There amidst those long,
trailing flags commemorating the lost world, among the
prism spectrums of silk windsocks, the dervish swirl of
kites and an occasional aquamarine bat, I moved, powered
only by air, and the pollinator appeared, aerial, before me.
We reached for each other the way birds swoop together.
And when the dance was over, we retired to my bower.
There we practiced a flight more fleshy, sprawling across
damp earth, drinking each other for water.

He'd grown up in the rain forest preserve. His parents
worked there, keeping alive what species they could.
They'd rocked him in a hammock slung amidst leaves,
bathed him in pools where jaguars drank. He made the
rounds with them, helped them keep up the undergrowth,
cultivate the essential fungi. He knew every bird, and
repeated with his parents the prayers for the flourishing of
insect populations. And when from time to time the multi-
nationals sent their raiders, the pollinator helped his
mother and father devise sabotage—sand in a fuel tank,
microbes in the drinking water, spikes hidden in the
trunks of the satinwood trees.

We were busy all through the velvet night, until first light lit the horizon. Then we slept, his chest against my back, his right arm around me, hand holding my secret nest.

The pollinator stops. We whisper, though there's no one to hear. There are only a few secrets left, and we're keeping them. Someday the Divenet may come back, or a new bird or moth fall in love with the Ooallecia. In the meantime the pollinator kisses my face, little kisses. He looks into my eyes for confirmation. Now we slip on the harnesses, get the rope ready. This is the steep part, up this cliff of uluhe, through violets vining the halas' trunks. Hold by hold we flit upward, quantum and fluid. I can see the blossom above us, nodding on its stalk. Beside me this man, a stream of blue vibrations. He is water and a little flesh, breathing. We are energy, and we never stop moving. We smell like sea salt, hand over hand, to the flower's lip.

Before the mercenaries took over, there were plenty of sweet boys. I used to find one, seduce him, then tear him to pieces. There were bumper crops, and everything worked the way it was supposed to. Now I offer myself to the soldiers, but they can't get it up. They tear each other to pieces, but the seeds wither in the ground.

I may be divine, but if the seeds don't grow, I won't be around much longer either. Not production but produce is the word: root, stem, blossom. You know my many names, their syllables resounding down through history, names like a cascading lustrum of water. Now my kingdom has diminished to this pinnacle, in the ether above this island afloat in the sea. But do your mourning for savannahs, lakes, jungles. Mourn the wetlands. Do not mourn for me.

This is the moment toward which we've climbed. Now from the vial attached to his belt he lifts the tiny wand, dips it into the Ooallecia's crevice. Then he leans across the flower and kisses me. I am here to make the pollen take.

We have to hurry. The Divenet knew this instinctively, and flew from flower to flower in a frenzy. The pollinator and I have thirty-six hours to reenact our wedding at each of the eleven other shrines. Our vow not to each other but to the Ooallecia.

This is the man I've looked for all my life.

HOW TO
ACCOMMODATE MEN

"You picked up the wine?" A asks me at breakfast. He leans on his elbows, observing my cleavage as I bend to check the muffins in the oven. I am wearing my see-through Renaissance robe with Juliet sleeves, the one A ordered for me from Night-and-Day Intimates.

"Wine?" I say, testing the muffins with a toothpick.

"For the party."

"Party?"

"The party for Subovsky." He sips his coffee slowly. Mornings he's slow. "A few people are coming over after Subovsky's talk. Not many, I'm keeping it small. I thought I told you. Did you forget?"

I never forget. I write things down. Even when I don't write things down, I don't forget. I didn't forget, but I don't say this. It would be counter-productive, and I'm geared for production.

"Maybe I did," I say. "I probably did."

"Not more than twenty," A says. "Wine and a few snacks. And get a bottle of Scotch too. Subovsky likes Scotch."

A few snacks, I think, bringing on the muffins. I can dash to the store during my lunch hour, if I time it right.

Eat crackers and nuts and yogurt in the store while I shop. And while I prepare dinner I'll make a paté. A likes an elegant surprise.

"Napkins," I say. "I'll get some paper napkins." A chews a bite of muffin thoughtfully while I rush to get a pad and pencil. Someone had better make a list, and it had better be me. Twenty means forty plus. They bring their wives and girlfriends, they invite an acquaintance at the last minute. Subovsky will have a local girl or two in tow. I'll get three Scotch and some gin and tonic too. Club soda, I think. Club soda and limes.

"Club soda and limes," A says. He gets up and goes to shower and dress.

I write down limes. Toothpicks. Small paper plates. Olives and salted nuts, a tray of cold cuts and cheese. Forty means mud on the carpet and wine stains, but the carpet needs cleaning anyway. I make a note to call the cleaning service and set up an appointment. I'll vacuum, I think, while the paté bakes. Clean the bathroom. Bring out the ashtrays. And pick up aspirin for the ones who think ahead to their hangovers.

I rush around in my head as I dress, thinking of everything. Thinking of everything is my specialty. Stamina is my specialty. I get by on very little sleep, and I can eat anything. Or I can eat next to nothing, if that's what there is. I have the constitution of an ox, though I don't look like an ox. I admire my handsome face in the mirror, my full head of hair, my Simone Signoret mouth. I'm a looker, with plenty of body. A likes body, as long as it's in the right places, and the right places are another of my specialties.

"I'm going," A calls. I hurry out of the bathroom to see him off. He likes to be seen off, and I don't disappoint him. On the stand I notice his library books, overdue. He's forgetting them again. I make a note to drop them off and pay the fine on my way to work.

"Keys?" I say.

Suddenly he's worried. He pats his pocket. Then he smiles. "I've got them," he says proudly, and kisses me. I flick my tongue in his mouth, quick quick, a little reminder of things to come. A likes to be reminded. His eyes register my reminder, and then he prepares himself. To get ready for *out there,* where it's hell, he goes chilly. He focuses on something distant and above me.

"Bye," I say, holding the door open for him.

On the third step he pauses and turns back.

"Ice," he says.

My smile is tropical.

"Ice," I reply.

When a man comes on to me, I help him. "Poor baby," my mother said when her man couldn't find his socks which were in his drawer or his nail clippers which were in his pocket. "They need our help," my mother said. This was the message I drank down with my mother's milk. A man has only to look at me suggestively and I'm thinking, oh where can I take him, where can I lay him down? One raised eyebrow and I'm off, I'm at his service.

I am never aggressive in traffic. On planes I give men the window seat. I give them my *Wall Street Journal.* I give them my piece of cake. In supermarkets I let men get in line ahead of me. And I carry in the groceries myself and put them away before A gets home. I feel out what a man wants and then I give it to him. And I always, always keep my conversation clean. I don't muddy the waters with unpleasant hints that he needs self-improvement or reminders to take out the trash. I take the trash out for him.

I never ask A where he's been. I don't challenge his extenuating circumstances. I treat his extenuating circumstances as his inalienable right. It's my specialty to make allowances for extenuating circumstances. And I fill his chinks with little appreciations of his male prowess and his talent for leadership. "What a stud," I whisper in his ear. "You ought to be senator."

At the office I get the work out. I don't miss work. I don't get sick. Getting sick as a general rule throws a wrench in things. It inhibits thinking of everything. It inhibits stamina. And it gives the impression of being unreliable. Mr. Washburn knows he can rely on me, and he rewards me with regular raises, bonuses at Christmas and on my birthday, and with his expensive admiration. I say expensive because he is stingy with admiration. No one else at the office gets any. There can only be one favorite at the office, and I'm it.

Mr. Washburn thinks he admires me because I'm efficient. *She gets the work out* is how he refers to the effect I have on him. He doesn't understand that it isn't what I do but who I am that has the effect of making his work, and his life, seem easier. Simply being in my presence makes everything seem easier to Mr. Washburn. General progress through the working day seems easier. Thinking of what to say in dictation seems easier when I take dictation. Getting up and getting showered and shaved and dressed in the mornings seems easier to Mr. Washburn, knowing I'll be there.

I make things seem easier than they actually are.

I have been with Mr. Washburn long enough that I no longer have to do the things I did at first. And I should add that I add an extra touch which Mr. Washburn is unaware of: I do not tempt him. Though I'm a handsome woman, I dress for work with a studied dowdiness. My clothes appear to be expensive but mute. My makeup is carefully keyed to erotic effacement. I wear my hair in a dowager's knot, and I appear to be without a waist. I look like a drudge, which enhances the impression that I get the work out.

And I never sit where Mr. Washburn can see my legs. I take it to my credit that Mr. Washburn has no idea how old I am. It has never occurred to him even to wonder.

Twenty is forty. I'm prepared. I can handle forty. I can handle sixty, I've tripled the recipe. I circulate among the guests, emptying ashtrays, sumptuous with preparedness. I can rein myself in or give myself full play. Be loosely flexible or graciously austere. Gay or elusive or intimately chatty. I'm prepared for the demands of the situation, and when the situation changes, I'm prepared for change.

A keeps Subovsky's glass filled, and I attend to the other forty-nine. I fill their glasses, and they confide in me. X confides he's having problems at work. He explains these problems in considerable detail. I nod sagaciously. My brow furrows ever so slightly, just enough to imply a womanly concern. I beg him to clarify the parts of his story which are still vague. I assure him I want the whole picture. Since I know the other men he refers to, I can agree, knowingly.

"Yes," I say, "you're right about Martin. Yes, he can be trying. Though you're right, he's unaware of this. And the fact that he's trying and unconscious of this fact makes it all

the worse, of course. Your judgment is absolutely accurate."
X begins to look happier. He becomes more animated. He
considers me an outside party. He feels I am an intelligent
but disinterested observer. He can trust my reaction to be
objective. And now I have vindicated his views. He feels
confirmed. He thinks me a remarkable woman, and his
respect for his colleague A clips up several notches.

I fill his glass and move on to Y. Y is disconsolate. I
attempt to cheer him up, but he won't be cheered. I inquire
discreetly into the cause of his gloom. He confides he's having problems at home. His wife has turned sullen, and his
children are becoming unmanageable. I sympathize with
the scourge of sullen wives and difficult children. I suggest
possible causes, I have a bagful of possible causes handy.
And I offer possible courses of action. I have quite a number of those on hand too.

Y deliberates. No, none of my suggestions will quite do
the trick. I offer yet another, brightly. Y deliberates again.
I attend his deliberation. I'm prepared to offer him my
attentive presence for as long as it takes. He considers at
length the advantages and the drawbacks of my last suggestion. At last he decides. He ought to have thought of it
himself, he says. In fact he had thought of it, but hadn't
quite countenanced his own ingenuity. Now he believes it's
a stroke of genius. He thanks me for reminding him of what
he knew all along was the solution. He beams. He is filled
with admiration for his own resourcefulness.

Now Z approaches me. His problem is epistemological. I
throw practicality to the winds. We are in the rarified
upper atmosphere and there is no telling when we will get
back down. But I don't worry. I let him fly the plane: I'm
along for the ride. He whisks me high above the abstract
scenery. Herds of *ifs* and *thens*, coveys of *howevers*. Flocks

of *it-would-seems*. Now we hover above the watering hole where at sunset these species converge.

Suddenly Z spots an opening in the tight circle around Subovsky. In the midst of a *nevertheless* he takes off. He flies away, but I do not fall to earth. I'm prepared for anything, especially for abrupt changes in elevation. I can glide along indefinitely, I can fly upside down, I can land on a dime. Humming, I wipe up a spill. A stays at Subovsky's side. I do a last minute check on the well-being of those who have not been able to command Subovsky's ear.

And then A asks me to drive Subovsky to his hotel. Subovsky is smart and smooth. He recognizes, when he meets me, that he's met his match. He asks me to come up for a nightcap. When I get back, the party is emptying out. The last guest leaves at 1:00 A.M., but A is still full of vim and vigor. Though it's late, he's been overstimulated. He's high on Subovsky's attention. He does not ask what took me so long. Instead he paces, unseeing, amidst half-empty glasses set down on the carpet, overflowing ashtrays, scattered paper plates. He needs a climactic end to the evening. Without it he will not be able to come down.

I'm prepared. I've got a reserve tank saved especially for A, and I know what he needs. I go to him wearing an expression of passionate intensity. I let him look into my eyes. I let him kiss me on the mouth. I let him think what he's thinking. He's thinking Subovsky. He's thinking how Subovsky took a certain, clearly discernible interest in him. How Subovsky seemed genuinely curious about A's work. How Subovsky recognized the perspicacity of A's casual remarks and laughed twice. How Subovsky followed A's line of argument thoughtfully and pointed out only two weak suppositions. How it's a sure thing that Subovsky will publish a chapter of A's new work-in-progress in his highly respected journal. And will pay tribute to A's shrewdness by recommending him for one of those grants you can't apply for. And will invite A to chair a panel next year at the international meeting in Prague.

I take A by the hand and lead him into the bedroom. I don't say a word. It might be counterproductive to interrupt his train of thought. He has just remembered that, among his many talents, is the fact that he's a hot hit with women. He remembers when he first swept me, so to speak, off my feet. How I was unable to withstand the smoldering of his sexual aura. One thing leads to another, and he remembers what a skillful lover he is, how capable he is of heavy-duty and prolonged performance. How his wide experience has inevitably made him adept at pleasing women. And how surprised they are when he knows in-stinctively what they like.

I lay him down and kneel between his thighs. My technique is surefire. I am swift and deft. I keep an eye on A's face and monitor his progress, its advances and retreats, its falterings and its holding steady. I tease him out, I get him to the first level and keep him there, then I bring him along a little further. When I've got him to the edge of the first level, I go ahead, I get him up to the next. Hand over hand, up we go. I know when to string it out, and when to speed toward the finale. I am sure of each hold, I know the way by heart. I know A by heart, his strong suits, his weak points. I have him plotted, and I have all the time in the world.

With me he's guaranteed the summit.

With me he can't fail.

I don't invite my mother to visit. I visit her, or I arrange to meet her somewhere else.

When A's mother comes, A is nervous and irritable. He has never been able to strike the right note with her. Though he says in his heart he loves her deeply, he has not succeeded in establishing satisfactory rapport. His mother's visits keep him a constant shambles. He can't enjoy his coffee at breakfast, and he can't concentrate on his work. At night he can't sleep.

She arrives with a walker, a bedpan, and her own special chair. Her go systems are liberally supplemented with hose and tube. I say I'll take over. I assure A I enjoy her company. She is sharp as a tack, and she doesn't miss a thing. She scolds me if the toilet needs cleaning, and she reads A's notes for his work-in-progress and pries into his calendar.

"Who's this Michele?" she demands. "Who's Rosalie?"

A puts his head in his hands. "No one you know, Mother," he says weakly.

"Michele is the dentist," I tell her. "Rosalie is his typist."

A and I lie in bed at night and whisper. Though she is deaf, she hears our voices. "I know you're talking about me," she calls out from the guest room. And she has an ear cocked for any rhythmic murmurings of the mattress. A lies beside me, flat on his back, rigid. He grinds his teeth. He groans.

"Do something," he begs me. "Think of something."

I get up and give her her pills. I get her to swallow them with a shot of Wild Turkey. I talk up whiskey as a time-tested, homeopathic remedy.

"This is not one of those newfangled horror drugs," I tell her. "Whiskey is reliable. It's been known for its healthy properties since ancient times. Mothers gave it to their babies when they were teething. Pioneer women used it, and it got them all the way West."

A's mother is impressed by what she perceives as my respect for the old, my distrust of the new. She beams up at

me from her bed jacket. I fill the glass again. "Drink this,"
I say.

Soon she's asleep. I take the whiskey and the glass back
to our bedroom. A is sitting up in bed, a wreck.

"I've put her to sleep," I say.

"What if she wakes up again?" he says. "She always
does. She never sleeps more than ten minutes at a stretch. I
won't get any sleep at all tonight."

I lean over him, holding the shot glass.

"Drink this," I say, handing him the glass. He drinks it
down. "She was asleep when I left," I say, filling the glass
again. "She won't wake up."

"I won't be able to sleep and tomorrow will be hell," A says,
downing the Wild Turkey. "How will I get through the day?"

"Trust me," I say, pouring one more. "You're going to
sleep all night. You're going to sleep like a baby. You're
going to wake up rested tomorrow. Tomorrow you'll feel
great. Just drink a little more of this," I say.

Men like having money.

I never lend A money. I never remind A I have money. A
assumes my salary is spent on clothes, the hairdresser, magazines. He assumes I make less money than I do, pocket
money. We don't discuss money, and A does not think of
money when he thinks of me. He has never seen me writing a check or paying the paper boy. He imagines my purse
holds Kleenex, lipstick, a mirror. I hide my checkbook and
my credit cards in a secret pocket, just in case he looks in
my purse for a book of matches.

Though I buy the groceries and pay the rent, it does not
seem so. The groceries seem simply to appear, and if we run
out of butter—but we don't. We'll never run out of butter.

A believes he supports me. A goes to the liquor store and buys a case each of scotch, bourbon, gin. He feels like a big spender. When he pays the cashier, he feels responsible. When he buys a tie or a suit, when he fills the tank of his Subaru, he imagines he's seeing to my welfare. He thinks he's thinking of me. He feels protective and generous, signing the receipt.

What I do is pay a part of A's bills on the sly. I pick bills he won't miss, charges he would rather forget: the opthomologist, the shrink, his account at the Wine Cellar, at *Logos*, at Subaru Sales and Service. I am careful never to pay off an account—that he would notice. Instead I slip in a payment here and there, middle sized payments, not enough to arouse suspicion, but enough to make his monthly statement a pleasant surprise. He imagines it is his own occasional payments that do this, or that he has actually spent less than it seemed. I make partial payments to Mastercard and American Express as well, and at the end of the month A discovers he has extra cash. Extra cash makes him feel expansive. He buys me three-dozen roses. He buys me a naughty black lace teddy. He buys me a cockatoo. And he takes me out to dinner five nights in a row. I lose two pounds and A gains ten. The waiters are impressed by the tips he leaves. Now he is out of cash, but he still has that rich feeling, so he makes a down payment on a tape deck for the Subaru and opens an account at Inner City Tapes and Records. He orders prescription sunglasses. And he puts a case of champagne on his account and charges a dozen new hardbacks.

The next day he comes walking in like Menelaus back with the booty. He's bought me an emerald bracelet he noticed I'd admired. I am astonished, overwhelmed.

"Oh!" I say. "You didn't! You shouldn't have!"

There is the faintest glimmer of the beginning of tears in my eyes. I put on the bracelet. I seem still overwhelmed, but A waves away my gratitude.

"There may be other little presents you'd like," he says. He suggests I make suggestions. I mention a suit I put on lay away at Bergdorf-Goodman's. A coat. Boots. I mention a car phone, some luggage. A bikini I tried on—he was with me, he remembers the bikini. A makes a note of the other things I've mentioned. He's into providence now, and profligacy. And he becomes suddenly protective. I should be cautious, he tells me, especially at night. He looks me in the eye to make sure I get his message. Park only in well-lit areas, he tells me. Then he revises this: if I need to go out at night, from now on he'll drive me, he'll pick me up at the curb. He feels generous, he feels flush, he feels extravagantly possessive. He strides back and forth, commanding space, dominating time.

In bed A is spunky and gymnastic. He wants to try every imaginable position. He insists on plying me with techniques. He becomes a veritable Book of Knowledge, and he wants his aerobic fitness confirmed.

"Like it?" he asks.

"Ummm," I say, purring.

"How about this?"

"Fantastic!" I say.

When he whips out surprises, I'm surprised. When he hopes to overwhelm me, I'm overwhelmed. The big spender is more work than the aspiring scholar, but I've got stamina. I'm prepared. And when A falls asleep, I balance my checkbook. I'm in the black.

Everything is going according to plan.

A is leaving me.

You might think I would be frantic. I'm not. When he announces he's moving out, I pretend to be surprised. He wants to surprise me. He thinks I haven't noticed his restlessness and the scent of perfume—not mine—on his skin. And he thinks Rosalie's new fervor, increased attentiveness, and her offer to let him stay at her apartment are the result of his own irresistible attractiveness.

"Oh!" I say, my face in lovely—but not too lovely—confusion. A does not like to feel conflicted. And A does not like scenes. They irritate his peptic ulcer. They interfere with his work. They play havoc with his sleep patterns and generally disrupt his *Weltanschauung*. He gets headaches. He gets pain in his shoulders. He gets distracted and forgets to record his checks or put money in meters. And he leaves the Subaru's lights on all night.

I am careful to avoid scenes. "You're unhappy," I say, my lower lip beginning to tremble. A looks down at the floor. When he looks up, I begin to weep, quietly. Then I withdraw discreetly to the bedroom, as though I need to think this over. I close the door behind me with exaggerated care, as though, with his announcement, all things in the material world have become inexplicably fragile.

A is relieved. He wants his departure to have an effect, but not so much that he need feel guilty. I give it to him just the way he wants it. I am careful not to upset him, and anyway, I'm not upset. I'm not angry, I'm not desperate, and I'm not surprised.

I lie down and pick up the book on my side of the bed and begin chapter twenty-two. Tonight I don't have to prepare dinner. I don't have to vacuum while the paté bakes. I don't have to fill glasses and empty ashtrays, draw out A's tedious colleagues, fly upside down and land on a dime. If I'm out of butter, it's no disaster—but I'm not out of butter. There's plenty of butter, and I am not the one who has to pack the bags, box the books, sort the medicine cabinet and the dirty laundry, find the wristwatch, the wallet, the checkbook, and the missing umbrella.

Day after tomorrow I fly to Tahiti. Mr. Washburn's travel designer has arranged my three week vacation with pay. I'll spend the first week there being wined and dined by Subovsky, enjoying my black lace teddy, my bikini. Then Subovsky will have to get back to work, and I'll spend the next two weeks bathing in the turquoise waters, admiring the emerald bracelet's shimmering in tropical twilight. When I return, tanned and rested, I may lie fallow for a while, avoid romantic attachments. I will live with the cockatoo for a while. Eventually though, I'll probably look for a replacement for A. It won't be difficult to find one to my liking. There are As out there like you wouldn't believe. Forty-nine percent of the population is male, and they all need someone to triple the recipe. They need someone to make allowances for extenuating circumstances. They need someone to think of everything, and they need someone to make 68 cents every time they make a dollar. They need someone to help pay their bills. In a word, *accommodation*. They've become dependent on accommodation, as much of it as they can get.

What do I get out of this? I know everything that's going to happen before it happens. I know because I make it happen. Nothing catches me off balance; there are no surprises. It's my hand on the tiller, me at the wheel. They don't move an inch I haven't foreseen and set in motion. They don't blink unless I set them blinking. They don't zip, they don't unzip.

When I finish chapter twenty-two, I begin chapter twenty-three. I'm in no hurry, I feel no anxiety, I'm under nobody's gun. It's A who will be distraught the next time his mother comes to visit. And when he discovers that Rosalie doesn't cook and has never emptied an ashtray. When Rosalie runs out of butter. And when he realizes how much it costs to keep Rosalie and how tricky it is to meet Michele three times a week without Rosalie finding out. And when the bills come in from Mastercard and American Express, when he suddenly discovers he's overdrawn.

And when Subovsky does not publish an excerpt from A's work-in-progress in his highly respected journal.

When the grants are announced, and it turns out Subovsky didn't after all recommend him.

When Subovsky does not invite A to chair a panel at the international meeting in Prague.

When Subovsky meets A between sessions in the corridor and passes him as though they've never met.

GLAMOURPUSS

I am Gloria Innanna Aphrodite Hapshepsut Jones, and I have been interested in glamour as far back as I can remember. It has little to do with men directly, though from the first I've been interested in them for cyclic purposes. As a baby I dreamily observed little boys from my mother's shopping cart, indulged a pleasant dalliance with certain ones in sandboxes. We sifted the sugary grains through our fingers, mumbling our singsong phonemes and sibilants, busy burying our legs, adding now and then a fistful to the other's embankment.

They seemed friendly enough companions, but my primary interest was me. I was busy distinguishing the swelling and subsiding enterprise I was from my surroundings. I idled in the bodily feel of things, mouthing my mother's nipple, feeling the filmy garment of summer air. I dawdled with Mother in the bath's effusion of bubbles, noting the camellia scent of soap, spreading its slick perfume on my skin. Afterward, toweled, I liked staying close to her, lulled by her sachet, braced by the astringent scent of her toenail polish. I liked to bury my face in her lingerie. And in the garden she sat me up near her lavender bush, where I rocked in the sun, tracking the tiny wavelets of my being. I was flowery mist, and nature a place of damp shine. Wherever I turned, pastel pulsations leaned in.

One day I reached and plucked a low peach. I peeled back the fruit's skin, sniffed, put the flesh to my mouth. The taste was a liquid sweetness, mixed with the humus smell of earth. My body, as I ate, seemed pale green, a new shoot about to open.

The picture books were portraits of me as my own ancestor. Isadora Duncan in her slow whirlwind of scarves. Nefertiti, regal, peacock feathers in her crown. Cleopatra, breasts cradling the gold ankh. The necklaces of Isis, heavy with emeralds. The clamoring of breath as Coatlique descended, stone by stone, the pyramid at Tenochtitlán.

Glamourpuss, glamourpuss, the boys chanted. *Don't try to put one over on us.* We met them in drop-the-handkerchief, fox-and-geese, ancient rites enacted in circles. Boys focused on the spherical—the arcs of basketballs, baseballs, softballs. Holding these objects so global, so tactile, they frowned, sighting, aiming, and observing a little way off a girl twirling in her circle, or two of us lolling in grass. Girls were narcissists, preening, combing each other's hair. Sometimes a girl stepped into the revolving sphere of rope turned by two others and bounced there, showing herself off.

Alone, I imagined myself that storybook princess who lay down drowsily on a bed of roses. I collected in a basket the petals of my mother's blooms, pouring this bounty onto my bedspread. When it wasn't enough, I went next door, hoping old Mrs. Ostermeyer wouldn't notice. It was June, midmorning, and I was nine. Bees nudged the air around my pink fingers, and the Ostermeyer's cat rubbed against my ankle. When I'd gathered the last basketful and poured the petals on my pile, I undressed and lay down on my back. The petals were cool. I sighed, I lounged, I lifted handfuls of petals and let them fall onto me. My skin seemed to give off a faint trilling.

Then I was twelve, and with blood came the tug of my calling. I imagined an extension of my glamour outward, an enlarging of this Botticellian planet. I would float on this buoyant ocean of being, tasting the body's salt on my tongue, but there would be perks: a boy would be there with me. He'd be slender, a dancer, capable of imagining a green pond's cotillion of lily pads. There we might float on the lazy fever of damp and dappled. I imagined two swans, one black, one white, long necks twining, heated hearts beating in duet.

My first was a grocery boy sprinkling produce. On an errand with my mother, I discovered him among the lettuce. My eyelashes were as long as the dragging tails of peacocks. It was December, seventh grade, and my breasts had just appeared. I lifted two leafy heads, one in each hand, and let him look at me. Then I bore the lettuce away, to my mother. After Christmas came Algebra, this boy and I seated side by side. He was X, I the center of a sky blue zero circle skirt. We finished our equations, then tic-tac-toed, X meeting zero over and over.

He played clarinet, reedy instrument needing a willing mouth. I became a majorette. But it was night we longed for, day merely a passage of sun until dark opened. We reclined in the plush back row of the theater. While the throat of a starlet rose hugely above us, we kissed, redefining those borders the makers of underwear take for granted. Around us dark hummed and swayed. Time spread its red esplanade.

My boy stayed sweet, without malice or greed, interested only in my pleasure. Any other girl might have settled down. But mine was not to stir a pot and populate the planet with cute offspring. My work depends on not attaching. I'm the one who comes, then goes. I plump up wildlife, nurture flora, patrol the perimeters of the realm. Fructifying was the trade I was learning, but now that I'd got the first part down, it occurred to me step two might be harder. When I understood this, daffodils were pushing spring. I had dallied on that bed of roses without responsibilities. Now I'd have to assume throne and scepter. It was my job to pick and choose, to send some men left and some right to their fates.

If my boy had known, he'd surely have resisted. And I didn't want him to suffer. I did it as it should be done, swiftly and brutally, without announcement. One dawn dripping with lilacs and dew, I ripped out his heart for the good of the polis. Then I went my appointed rounds, sprinkling his blood through the wheat, corn, barley.

I wept, but not long. A glamourpuss can't afford to. There are always more seasons, one after another, and you have to keep them coming. Boys think of glamour as a substance with magical properties, one they can't manufacture themselves, a kind of girlish endorphin. Most are eager to come under its sway. A track star lasted six months before planting time came around with Jupiter. I returned his class ring, sopping up the blood with his letter sweater as best I could, wringing it out over those nubile furrows. When I'd matriculated I traveled abroad, took up with a Nepalese student in Prague, and the following spring the son of the Japanese ambassador. The year after, I chose a young Persian lawyer, then a Burmese bureaucrat whose mouth resembled a sea cucumber. There was a Hungarian cellist I was sorry to select, and an engineer or two, though they are usually over-scheduled. Generally I avoid the military, but one Mongol lieutenant preferred pacifism and was too shy to say so. And one spring, I'm proud to say, I saved a Green Beret from anonymous death in the foliage of Asia. Better the fertilizing of organic produce, I reasoned, than programmed slaughter in the service of petroleum and hubris.

I liked best the slender ones, the ones like saplings, blond or bronze or ebony, it didn't matter. The bold and the shy, the ambitious and the lazy, the sleek and the craggy, the brooding and the boisterous. All offered themselves, breathless and gleaming, like salmon hurling their bulk into higher light. I noted their innocence, admired the way they filled out muscle, but in the end I could not keep any of them. They were all grist for the glamourpuss mill.

Then Aelf. He came to me in Alexandrian summer. We still believed such seasons were not aberrations, that the fine foam of June air would continue to precede July's extravagant foliage. But the devastation had begun. The great ice caps had begun to trickle, and the number of heat waves in temperate zones shot up. Those of us who'd dallied for aeons in rain forest dapple knew. These green spinnings could not spin on.

Day by day there were more Australians with sunburns. Day by day there were fewer fish and fowl. I had my work to do replenishing the stock, and Aelf was slender, with eyes of emur. His instrument the bamboo lute. I was at that stage where things are soft and gaudy, bangle bracelets tinkling suggestively. I wore cloth of ocean, and my aura had no edge. Aelf watched me put up my hair with pins.

"Glamourpuss!" he teased. I pretended I was forced to it by custom. But he seemed to know the impulse was encoded, peach pit in each of my glistening genes.

We convened. His longing met mine. We formed an arc without decline while the surf beat out its varying rhythm, and late summer fell away toward September. Other lovers let go, but we held on, riding the flow and ebb of each second, savoring the soft edge of time's coming and going.

"Honey," he called me, because I slid. "Happy," he called me, for Hatshepsut, and kissed my hieroglyphic mouth. While blithe governments ran on like printers, spitting out the work of a cyber novelist, Aelf and I lay down in fallow furrows, fertilizing the slumbering fields. Sex was humus, each caress a carbon scented leaf, transparent, giving itself to layered sediment.

"Give me another swallow," Aelf would say, and I would. So we wallowed through winter, wound around each other, warming the shivering earth, blowing on its flame our combined breath.

Why this time did I become attached? Aelf's name became my mantram. I proceeded in studied denial, searching chronology for a way to keep him. My desperation became more frenzied as I tried to quell it. I was anxious, and for good reason: there is no hook and eye that holds. Ours is a universe on the loose, disappearing and reappearing thousands of times a second. To tie things down is dangerous, especially in my business.

I thought about this in the bath, amidst the bubbles' airy bursts. I heard the effervescent wisdom, but resisted. Why not let bliss drift? So I let it snow through April, and on the first of May produced a delicate spring blizzard. Light-filled flakes floated slowly earthward. I lay in our bower, my skin tangerine from our burnishing.

Aelf stood, brooding on the deluge. His lute lay on the comforter, silent. "The aubergine won't ripen," he said. "Your favorite. Why this lateness? I fear for us."

My heart fluttered. You cannot put this off, I thought. I lectured myself sternly, tried to gather resolution—but I could not sacrifice Aelf, not even for arugula and aubergine. This one I would save. But the only way I could think to save him was to leave him.

"Aelf," I said that night in bed. We lay spooned, my back to his belly, his hand over my nest. "You are destined to become a great inventor. I feel it."

"I don't know how," he said. "Anyway I'd rather be a cook or oversee a botanical garden."

"You must go to college."

"Never. They want all those students to crank out quicker war planes, bigger bombs. Not to mention new forms of white phosphorous, cyanide necklaces, and scatter pellets."

"Not those, no. You must invent a new, expensive—but not too expensive—toy. Something as much fun as a car but which doesn't require petrol or asphalt."

He perked up. "You'll come with me," he said.

"After a little while. But first I must go into the Peace Corps. I want to help the starving Somalis."

"So do I. I'll come along," he said. "We'll do college together after."

I put my hand where he liked it.

"We'll only be apart for a little while. You go start inventing. Soon I'll join you."

"Why this separation?" he said. "Is this a test?"

"Yes," I said. "A test of your love."

He smiled then, and kissed me. "I can pass it."

So I left, and left him alive. I was wretched, but it was May. I had to hurry. Blindly, I found some boy. Numb as I was, I could not tock his ticking, sniff the scent of his nooks and crannies. I managed, but it was sham, and while I performed this slam-bam, my heart curled up. I was a bound foot, walking myself through the ritual motions. When he fell asleep, I pulled from my purse Aelf's favorite satin sheet, steeped in our scent, worn threadbare by our plunging. The boy snored, and I held this shroud and sobbed.

By dawn I'd sprinkled the fields and gone.

The harvest that year was meager. Came then the maelstrom of famine. The Great Powers plumbed their coffers, but dearth of grain meant the death of many sweet children. There were flash floods and scorching burn, and the air became discernably bitter, and through the Indian subcontinent spread a fit of plague.

The tightly laced chill that had filled me loosened. I became the moan of a violin which rises up for a phrase, then plunges. I watched Aelf from afar. He had searched for me, scouring the Peace Corps' projects, wandering the world's lost beaches, stooped, brooding, finally dumb.

And I, I could do nothing.

Let the crystal glass be crushed, let this crown of hair fall down around me. Let lengths of black cloth be torn. I longed, alone inside my ashen gown. I held myself in my arms and rocked, while around me the green world went on with its denial, pulsing forth what pale shoots it could, egging out a few baby birds. All waterfalls and springs had not ceased, and these were heralded as signs of nature's inexhaustibility. But there was population everywhere you looked, elbowing for room, and bands of desultory gangsters with boom boxes roamed even the outermost ranges.

Wild quiet had become extinct.

They'd cranked up the power at great expense, hoping to fool themselves a little longer. No matter that the earth kept turning longingly toward dark: everywhere they set up glare. The savannah was like a used car lot at night, without the asphalt. Of that wide bolt—warp of dark, woof of quiet—there was now no remnant.

What animals were left couldn't sleep. The big cats, now lean, lay about, disconsolate. I met an elephant, trunk ripped in a wire snare—each time she drew up water to squirt into her mouth, most of it leaked out the ragged holes. She and I took a shine to each other, I leaned on her shoulder. She hung her head, I mine.

Then the fax. I should have known someone so finely strung as Aelf could not long endure the century without me. It seemed he'd gone back to college, but one day, as he stood on his balcony in the filthy air, he arrived at some final reckoning. I imagine him picking up the lute, holding it a moment, then laying it down. They say he'd bolted his door. I see him bring out the capsule he's constructed in the lab. I make myself watch him bite the glass and swallow.

It's hard these days to find an idle boy. Most are in uniform, or logged on and zoned out. When I lure one away from his monitor, he wants a quickie: double cheeseburger on the way to the stadium. It's as though the burgeoning world is a tedium. These boys have lost the cellular connection. Worst of all they don't often bathe, now that there's so little water.

The fields that once fed us are mined, or if not, then a blight of condos covers them. Now it's algae farms, shellfish in questionable brine, seaweed and plankton for the masses. The furrows in which I lay down like a silver thread of mercury are no longer plowed. They're under asphalt. Bits of cellophane wrapper, plastic pull tabs, crushed cigarette packs blow across the pavement.

What's a goddess girl without birds? How feel glamourous without beasts? I've lost quetzal, flamingo, lapwing, gull. The majesty of jaguars is gone, and the silver slide of narwhal and seal. Oh the orchards of peaches, sequoia and cedar! And meadows, their affairs with dew and sun—how dream without a supply of meadows?

When I can find a bath to run, I do, but I cannot long be comforted by water. Eventually I stand, towel off, talcum the crevices, get dressed and go out—but not into moonlight. In our jibbering illumination, I wander the ruins, imagining our lost soil, aerated by diligent worms, loose as a handful of unstrung pearls. Heart, my sister, reliable fire, you who have warmed me from the inside out down through the spiraling years, stop battering. Let me be!

But it goes on beating.

I'd like to call us to worship of the cycle, that uroboros snake with its tail in its mouth. I'd like to say I went tripping from dappled shade to sun-struck field, nourishing seed, bringing forth produce. But illusion is not voluptuous. Only reality has a body, lushly fleshed and decked out in freckles. Heart, my chime, it's April, it's time.

I slip the blade into the sheath strapped to my thigh, go out to where you can sense the line of a horizon. I have my drum, my rattle and flute, my feet and a beat in this bruised heart. I trek along, reciting my names, Gloria Innanna Aphrodite Hatshepsut Jones.

Let there be wine and more wine poured, and a bouquet of black rags and bones. And let there be crystal for the final swallow. I spread bleached linen on the ground, sit my pretty body down cross-legged. I position my blade, its edge thinned to a single row of electrons. I sing out the sequence of holy names, make the sign of the seven directions. Aelf, my beloved, yes: it's come to this. This time it's my heart I'll pry from its neat socket, lift, hot in my two hands, and wring, wet muscle, soaked sponge, over our abandoned ground.

THE
ISLAND

2

IRON SHARD

The cries of first birds with first light have passed. Dawn comes in billions of little pieces, stitches loosely sewn together, like breathing. Isn't the core of the sun iron? This sliver of iron in Radika's hand could have come from the sun, shot out of its heat through space like a bullet, embedding itself, becoming part of the earth.

From where she sits she can see the gate, and along the cadjun fence, the banana trees, ancestors gathered in council. Beyond the gate: more lanes, and the lagoon, a soft slapping, then the green of the sea, that mothering water, huge as the goddess herself. The mesh holds: green and gold, froth and foam. Radika feels the iron shard in her palm, and she is strong enough to think the forbidden thought: their mother isn't coming back.

Though at first the idea had been unthinkable, there came a time when the thought presented itself, almost shyly, a little waif of a thought at the edge of consciousness. It was only when Radika acknowledged its presence that this orphan grew to have substantial body. Now, the seventh day, she is ready to look into its eyes.

Six days ago, when she woke and saw blood on her nightgown, she'd tried—for a moment—to pretend she hadn't. Though bleeding marked an important passage, there was a saying. *If you see it first, it's a flaw, but if your mother sees it first, it's a good thing.* She'd hurried to where her mother slept, touched her shoulder, told her. Her mother turned over. Like one of those hibiscus blossoms slowly unfurling, sleep opened around her and she sat up and drew Radika into her arms.

"In seven days we'll have your ceremony! Remember when we did it for Sivarani?" Her sister Sivarani, of the black waterfall hair. At thirteen, she'd never cut it. It hung to her waist. She brushed it every morning and evening, as though each stroke down its strands was a prayer. Radika remembered Sivarani's excitement, how each of the six days of seclusion friends and relatives had come to offer congratulations. "You got to help serve sweets, remember? This time we'll let Maheswary help."

This blood, her mother had said, was not like the blood of bullets. It was good blood: a sign that from Radika's body could come a baby, out of almost nothing.

Later her mother had gone off to the market with her friend Praba. They'd made their purchases, and as they walked out beneath the arch, five Tiger separatists had appeared and surrounded them. The army checkpoint was only a few hundred yards away, but you couldn't see the market entrance from there. The Tigers liked to kidnap people right under the soldiers' noses. It made the army look ineffectual. Quickly, in spite of Praba's protests, they'd taken Radika's mother away.

Praba had come back to the house, carrying her mother's bag. Inside, some tomatoes, a bottle of oil.

Each day Praba goes to the Tigers' jungle headquarters, and each day the sergeant promises to release Radika's mother. Yesterday he'd promised absolutely: her mother would be back for the ceremony. But what he said, Radika thinks, is not the truth. He is like this time, which is not a good time. This is why Praba gave her the iron shard: to ward off evil. Her mother had given her the arica nut-cracker to hold, but later Praba brought this iron splinter—a bit of grenade? Or is it a sliver of metal from a mine? It would work, Praba insisted, because it had The Troubles in it. You used a piece of the evil against itself.

Radika sees the way the trees are there, rooted, leaves swaying above this rootedness, like women standing, intent on some task, humming to themselves. She imagines Praba at the market arcade, her hair a mane, scolding the Tigers. Why question the good woman who'd collected money for their cause, a woman whose son and daughter had themselves become separatists? But the one in charge had spit in the dirt at Praba's feet. And when she faced the sergeant, asking about her friend, he'd spoken bluntly. "Possibly she has kept some of our money for herself."

Radika imagines Praba shaking her great mane of hair. "Never in a thousand years."

Say the sun's a mother and the earth her daughter. Heat begins to swell, warming the sand, the way a mother's body warms you. Later the light will be white, heat rising from the sand in waves. If Radika could see the lagoon, it would look like a mirror laid along the edge of the town. The banana trees' leaves are wide fans, fringed along the edges, this fringe murmuring. The gecko on the stone step resembles a dry leaf.

The gecko is good at waiting, Radika thinks. And I am like him. Now Maheswary carries in the tray, sets it on the bed. Her small hands flutter around the bowls of rice, of dahl. "Is this enough?"

Radika kisses her sister's cheek. When Maheswary was born, Radika helped care for this baby as though she were one of its mothers. Their father had seemed to Radika merely an admiring presence, and Chilliyan and Sivarani were too old to be much interested. The baby smelled like flowers. Her softness resembled the softness of petals.

"You smell like jasmine," Radika says. She notices the fine hair on Maheswary's arms. Maheswary has never known a time without The Troubles. She's never been allowed to play outside after dark. Always there have been government soldiers on the streets and Tigers in the surrounding jungle, some of them boys not much older than Radika.

And yet Maheswary seems not to be afraid. Her exuberance resembles heat escaping from beneath the lid of a pot.

"I have to get your sari ready," Maheswary says. She darts to the door. "Don't leave the room!"

The iron shard is warm, as though just now burst off from its explosion. Their father had explained how The Troubles began, but Radika has forgotten. What she remembers is the story a school friend told her. In the capital, two sisters were walking home. Suddenly there was a crowd, men and women shouting, their shouts like stones flying through the air. One man kicked the eldest girl hard, and she fell. Then a woman grabbed the younger sister's hair and yanked her down.

So many shouts, each shout another stone.

Then the gleam of a machete. Two machetes.

Afterward two heads lay on the pavement.

The story had entered Radika suddenly, as though one of those shouts had hit her. She didn't know what to do with this story. She wanted to tell her mother, but it was not a good story. How could you ask about such a thing?

This land is the color of sand and dun cadjun, as heat from the sun is the color of lightning, as lagoon water is a slice of silver, too bright to look at long. The washerman's doty is white, a way of warding off heat. He comes through the gate, lays his stack of white cloths by the fence. Radika remembers when she felt safely surrounded by this fence, before three aunts and uncles moved across the strait to India.

The fourth aunt, her father said, had been given, unfairly perhaps, almost all the beauty in the family. Gazing at her was like drinking a glass of water when you were very thirsty. This aunt's husband, a doctor, had traveled to the capital for supplies. He'd been arrested by the army on suspicion of passing medicines to the Tigers. The aunt believed if she could get to the capital she could convince the brigadier to release him. It happened that the family next door was taking their son there, to send him to London to study. Radika's aunt paid bribes to get a pass, then set off on a bus with her neighbors.

When they got down to one of the checkpoints, the sentry had examined the aunt's pass, then taken her aside. He'd waved the others through, speaking in Sinhala. None of them could understand him. A jeep pulled up, and the sentry gestured toward the aunt with his rifle. She got in. He climbed in beside her, motioned the driver on.

Such a simple thing, driving away in a jeep. Radika imagined the jeep returning, bringing her aunt back. But her father, when he told them what had happened, did not say so. What he said was, "She was too beautiful."

If you could look directly at the iron in the center of the sun, would it resemble a god's shield, burning? But if there are gods, why shields? Is destruction a threat even to a god?

If iron keeps away the evil eye, you'd think fewer soldiers would die. But bullets and grenades don't protect soldiers. The government soldiers are supposed to protect people from the Tigers—not just Sinhala people, Tamils too—but these soldiers are like an occupying force. If they need to move troops, they commandeer the buses, and if they need space, they take over your house. And when the Tigers show their videos at the school, enticing boys and some girls to join them, this daring makes the soldiers furious. Then they carry out house-to-house searches, or arrest fishermen they suspect of aiding the separatists. At checkpoints they riffle through women's bags of rice, searching for weapons.

They do these things, and they speak in a language no one understands. At least the Tigers speak Tamil. And they're fighting for Eelam. Everyone wants Eelam, that heaven on earth. But Radika feels confused. Don't they have Eelam already? Aren't her parents, brother and sisters, their relatives and friends Eelam? If the government soldiers went away, wouldn't that be Eelam? The Tigers wouldn't have to fight then. They too would stop being soldiers.

The way it is now though, the Tigers act like the soldiers. They take a farmer's rice harvest, and sometimes don't pay. Once Radika watched two Tigers steal the clothes a woman had hung out to dry. Or several may appear suddenly in your doorway and demand that you cook a meal for them. If they need gas, they siphon petrol from your tank. Both the Tigers and the government levy taxes. Both sides make people passing on the road dig up mines. And both help themselves to girls. Just last week two girls left the high school as usual, and no one has seen them since.

When Radika was little, her brother Chilliyan used to swing her up against the sky, laughing. Chilliyan and his friend Vadevilu took her and Maheswary to the lagoon to skip stones and look for fish. Vadevilu had been welcome in their house, as Chilliyan had been in his. The boys were sixteen when some Tigers came to the school with videos. The videos showed boys advancing, rifles ready. One told how a cup of rice and a cup of water each day were enough, because it was for Eelam. And the Tiger girl who'd lost both arms spoke defiantly. She'd rigged her rifle so she could pull the trigger with her teeth. She stood, flanked, a girl fighter on each side, the empty sleeves of her shirt blowing in the breeze.

Both families had begged the boys not to join, but Chilliyan and Vadevilu insisted. The evening of Chilliyan's departure, their mother wept. But her anxiousness had not persuaded him to change his mind.

Afterward she'd offered to collect the Tigers' tax from the people in her ward.

"Don't try to dissuade me," she'd said to Radika's father. "It will help keep him safe."

"Maybe," he said. "But suppose you can't get as much money as they want? Or suppose someone decides to tell the soldiers what you're doing."

The washerman gets busy setting up the pantel that will shade the guests from the sun. Though it's early, Radika watches the gate. This is the gate through which their aunt walked away, the gate through which Chilliyan left them. And it was through this gate, one evening at dusk, that a band of Tigers came into the compound.

Their father had come from the telegraph office, then gone out back to bathe. He liked to shower with the hose as he watered the portulaca in the garden. Radika and Maheswary sat at the table, doing schoolwork. Their mother was setting rice to boil. She'd sent Sivarani to the market, despite her protest. Sivarani liked to be home when their father got there. Her love for him was like the equatorial weather opening thousands of water lilies. She brooded around him, bringing him little attentions, and she liked to accompany him to the temple where, in rites made puissant by repetition, he attended the goddess. It was as though Sivarani's gaze was an unbroken illumination in which she held their father up before them.

Radika's father came in wrapped in a sarong, humming a song Maheswary had taught him. He plucked a banana from the bunch, and, still humming, pulled back the peel and took a bite. Radika saw the Tigers first. One by one they stepped from the haze of dusk through the gate, each with his rifle pointed toward the doorway.

"Father," she whispered. He turned. There were nine. It seemed to Radika that her father was strangely unafraid. He held the banana before him like a taper, by the light of which those assembled might examine each other.

The Tiger boys formed a line. At their center stood Vadevilu. Later their mother would say his commander might have sent him as a test of loyalty. It was a thing soldiers did to each other. A current of air stirred the banana leaves so that their fringes rattled softly. Vadevilu stepped forward. He did not say her father's name, but he looked at him. "You have to come," he said. "It's because you operate the telegraph. The leaders think you've passed secrets."

Radika's father also stepped forward. "What secrets?" he said. "Question me. Ask."

Vadevilu shook his head. "Just come."

"Vadevilu," their mother said. She stood beside her husband in dusk light. "You know I collect the money."

Vadevilu shook his head. "This isn't to do with you. The leader wants your husband."

"What will Chilliyan think?" she said. "Look at this man: this is Chilliyan's father. Think what you do."

"Don't make trouble," Vadevilu said. He spoke as though furious at the necessity of having to speak at all. "Your husband has to come. It's an order."

Their father's back straightened, and Radika thought he was going to refuse. The banana in his hand could be a reason. If a man was eating, you didn't take him away, not then. But he turned to their mother and handed her the banana, as though in doing so he gave away his last possession.

When Sivarani came through the gate and across the sand, the banana lay on the table, one bite gone.

Perhaps the sun is not a god's shield, but the blazing countenance of the goddess. Isn't that why no one can look at it directly? See how she bares her shining throat! Bow down, open your mouth, utter the white hot syllables of asking. Bring fruit, bring garlands. Bring something alive. Give it into her fiery teeth. But if she is just, why doesn't she burn the bad ones, keep the innocent from burning? She's not so simple. She is peace in the water, conflagration in the atom. The opening, the closing, and everything between.

The washerman mounts the steps and walks through the rooms, chanting, sprinkling the floors with turmeric water. It's supposed to be women from your family who perform the bathing. At Sivarani's ceremony they came like a delegation, diplomats in saris, each carrying her water jar. The washerman filled each jar with sacred water. Each woman spread a white cloth over the jar's mouth. When it was time, the women rose as one body, as one body poured this water over Sivarani. Water, blessed, its lustrum a rush lifting you into the realm of grown women.

But the aunts and their families have gone across the strait, and the grandmothers won't be here either. One grandmother died before The Troubles. The other grandmother had visited them often. Radika liked to help this grandmother wash Sivarani's hair. In the cool of early morning Sivarani would appear, holding out the soap, the towel, the comb. "Please, Grandmother. Will you help me?" Then they went out to the spigot near the banana trees. Sivarani bent forward, and Radika and her grandmother began.

Women's hair was valuable, like gold jewelry. You let it grow. Sivarani had let hers fall around her like a queen's gown. Her hair had made her feel grown, and she'd acted as a grown woman might to find their father. She'd sent word to a girlfriend who'd joined the Tigers, and this friend had reported that she knew the camp where they kept him. Sivarani had gone with this friend, leaving in the night while the family slept.

A month had passed, and another month. One day before the monsoon began, they'd received a letter in Sivarani's handwriting. *I am a revolutionary now, like Chilliyan. I know how to make a land mine. We have to, to fight for Eelam. The Leader says there is no other way.*

The letter did not mention their father.

"Will Sivarani come back?" Radika asked. Her mother stood as though held by two strings pulling in opposite directions. "Maybe I shouldn't have collected money," she said. "It must have looked to Sivarani like I wanted to help them."

"She went after father," Radika said. Her mother did not speak. Mentioning their father was like the bad story. No one knew what to do with it. Radika remembers looking out into the compound, seeing the banana leaves swaying slightly. Their green resembled a slacking, water drunk down slowly, deliciously.

I have cut my hair, Sivarani wrote. *All the girls do it, to show we're loyal.*

Radika had never seen a Tamil woman who'd cut her hair. It wasn't done. She could see the spigot where they'd knelt so many times. The Tigers were supposed to be good Tamils. Why had they done this to the girls? How could such a thing be Eelam? Their mother had pulled Radika and Maheswary against her belly. Her hair fell around them, an airy veil.

Their grandmother had wept, and Radika and Maheswary and their mother had come around her. The four of their bodies, grieving, formed a mound. That was how you did it, and then, after a while, the grief was almost gone. But this grandmother persisted in grieving. As the weeks passed, Radika cast about for means to distract her— prayers, little love gifts, hopeful pleading. She'd lied the way adults lie to comfort children. Sivarani would return when the war was over, Sivarani's hair would grow long again.

But grief was a stone around which the old woman shrank like a drying fruit. Finally she had gone across the strait to her younger son, away from The Troubles. She lived there a while. Then one night while the others slept, she let go the thread of the world.

Father is dead, Radika thinks. Wasn't that why Sivarani hadn't written one word about him? And what but the certainty that Sivarani would never see her father again could have prompted her to pledge herself to the Leader, to cut her hair?

Sivarani won't come today because she doesn't know about Radika's ceremony. The grandmothers won't come either, nor will the aunts, uncles, cousins. Her mother had explained this on that first morning. Travel is too danger-ous now, and everyone has less money.

The sun is neither gleaming shield nor goddess' counte-nance, but the mound of a woman's belly, that round, red heat where flesh comes to fruition. Green, gold, leaves, heat, water. The gate of the body, the gate beneath the trees. They tell you you'll be happy with a husband, you will make your husband happy, and your strong body will make a good baby. What they don't tell you is the banana lying on the table, one bite gone.

Nor do they tell you the lamentation of hair slashed off, flung to the ground.

Now the washerman lays a white cloth across the cere-monial board: how bright, this slab of light where she will kneel. It occurs to her to wonder: should she keep holding the iron shard through the ceremony?

"Look, Radika, red!" Maheswary says, dancing in with the sari. Red, the color of the hot cries of parrots. The color of women's heat. Radika tucks in one end of the sari, then twirls, turning into Maheswary's winding. "Look! They're coming!" Maheswary points. Their mother's friends, by twos and threes, come through the gate, each woman with her jar. And here, across the sand, comes Praba. Mahes-wary's energy is a flock of tiny birds. "A red sari, Radika! And Mother's gold necklace, all for you!"

Because Maheswary reaches up to fasten the clasp of the necklace, Radika sees the lorry first. The driver, a girl about Sivarani's age, halts, keeps the motor running. Beside her, a boy in uniform with a rifle.

Another boy with a rifle leans out from the back.

Maheswary runs out of the room, flies across the sand to the gate. She and the girl speak. Then Maheswary hurries toward the back of the lorry. The banana trees suggest a graceful calm. The boy at the back bends down. Later Radika will remember how Praba, turning toward the lorry, had lifted her water jar onto her shoulder, as though ready to pour. She will also remember the sound that goes up from the women, the rush of air from a flock of birds beginning to rise, then falling back.

There in the dirt a rolled up blanket, a blanket with holes in it.

From the blanket's rolled edge a single foot protrudes.

The boy holds his rifle and looks down at Maheswary with the curious interest of someone engaged in a novel experiment who now observes the outcome.

Maheswary looks down. Their mother was a small woman with long feet that seemed to connect her securely to the earth. Radika remembers feeling safe walking beside her, observing how solidly those feet fit the sand. She sees Maheswary reach out, stroke this foot as though to soothe it.

It is all there: the green, the gold, the light, the heat, the sand an esplanade all the way to the gate, and beyond the compound the lagoon and the sea, benedictions of water spilling into the world. The lorry pulls away. Radika walks out onto the stone step. The gecko is gone. The space between her and the gate has taken on the aspect of terrain difficult to negotiate. She passes the washerman where he squats, a dumb tool. The women have collapsed against each other like jars thrown down, one or two cracked, broken. Radika hears Maheswary's weeping. She hears the barely audible ticking of the heat, the sound time makes, the sound of waiting and not knowing, of knowing but not knowing who, of knowing who but not knowing when, of knowing when but not how.

The truth is the sun is a burning star, and there are no favorites. Its gaze illumines soldier and civilian, enemy and friend, man and woman. The young and the old. The living and the dead.

Did their mother keep some of the money she'd collected for the Tigers?

She might have kept a little. Anyone might have. Enough to buy tomatoes, and some oil.

Maheswary's gaze rests on Radika, as though she imagines it was this sister's belly she slid from, as though, if she could, she would climb back inside. There may have been a time when iron kept evil away, Radika thinks, but that time is gone. Iron splinters and breaks apart: here's a bit of it, in her hand. She lets it fall onto the sand. The nature of iron has been changed by the violence with which men hurl it through the air. Now iron draws death toward you. Already a similar bit of iron may have sped toward Chilliyan and found him. Or toward Sivarani. There are many, many bits of iron flying through the air. It could have happened easily to both of them. Is the messenger even now hurrying toward them with the news?

THE FIRST
SENTENCE

They are alone on the verandah, Eve and Lallith, slice of
light laid next to a slice of shade. Leaves, green platters,
suspended beyond the railing. They are guests in the
house, their hosts gone out. Siva to his office, his wife Mani
on some errand. Probably to buy white bread, Eve thinks.
Eve doesn't especially like the bread, but it's prized here by
the middle class.

Awwwk of crows on the roof. This is Lallith's country,
though he's moved his family—wife, nine-year-old daughter, small son—to a northern European nation. Flecks of
gray in his black bush of hair. Eve has not seen him smile.

—Please, you will show me photos of your paintings,
Lallith says.

The formality of his sentence sets Eve at a distance.
Don't judge, she thinks. His oils have received a distinguished prize in that European country. They have painting in common, and around this they may forge—what?
Friendship? Kinship? He knows some English, though his
command of it is crude. Still, in his own tongue he may be
eloquent. She knows only a few words of Tamil. When she
utters them, they're a strange taste in her mouth.

From her bag, photographs: bright hues, her sensuous, palpable people, their faces melting into splayed foliage. Her mother, old, softened. A child, oblivious amidst toys. A woman bathing children, tub of water in the green light of lime trees.

—You do not abstract expressionist, Lallith says.

Compliment or critique?

—No, she says. —I like the shapes and textures of what I see: plants, people, this shiny tricycle.

He studies the tricycle. Weighing? Feigning interest? Eve can see motes floating in sunlight. Was that green streak beyond the railing a parrot? Sound of a hawker outside, calling out in Sinhala or Tamil—which is it?

—Technique is very good, he says.

Does he mean brush stroke? Composition? The few English words they share seem fuzzy, indefinite. Siva had pointed out Lallith's painting on the dining room wall. Severe, Eve thought. Hard lines—except for that swirling mass of softened red near the lower left corner. Now Lallith tells her a foreigner saw his paintings, arranged a scholarship in that northern country at a time when his life was in danger.

—She saves me for no reason, he says. Did he mean to say *he?* He'd accepted the scholarship, and once there, he'd been offered a job by a government organization. The organization testified that his expertise on South Asia was essential to the nation. This had set him up for citizenship.

—So I move my family away from The Troubles.

Did that mean a troubled marriage as well? But the war had split thousands of families. Men sent wives and children abroad, parents sent offspring. Lallith, Siva told her, had been student leader at the Tamil university. He'd been a rebel leader too, before things got bloody and the papers started calling the rebels insurgents. Some Tamils fled to the capital then, hoping to get their sons and daughters passports. Now there are a hundred thousand refugees from this war. Or expats, Eve thinks, depending on their class, caste, wealth.

She thinks of aborigines' songlines, how each line comes out of a particular place in the earth, how when a person is born his being comes from that place, so that those lines become his to carry. He can take you to that place, show you where the lines come out of the ground. Imagine being forbidden to return to that place: is this why Lallith won't smile? His hands, a child's fat fingers on a man. And his body, stocky, thick. She guesses he's not a good dancer. With his wild hair and big teeth, he seems part ape. Though he's made attempts at gallantry, banter. Siva, that morning, had brought her a handful of dharma blossoms from his walk in the garden. She'd floated them on water in a rice bowl.

—You are practicing flower arrangement? Lallith had said, a serious expression on his face.

She'd been startled. Was his remark an attempt to amuse her? If so, why hadn't he smiled?

She tries to imagine him with a brush, canvas, far off in that northern country. What are his other paintings like? The one on Siva's wall might be an anomaly, uncharacteristic of his newer work.

—Is this move to Europe permanent? Temporary?

He shrugs. —I will visit. I miss my son. But I am not patient in another country. Here is suffering, and I am responsible. I have to work to make it stop.

Eve nods. But why does he miss only his son? Had he meant to suggest he missed them all, but most of all his son? Now the temple gong: our task in this life is to pay attention. Lallith speaks now about his wife, how, in this culture of arranged marriages, she'd courted him. The young woman had appeared out of nowhere: they'd had no friends in common. But she'd been studying him. She'd presented herself, proposed that they marry within seven days. She'd wanted to present the marriage as a fait accompli. Then her parents couldn't make a counterproposal.

Sun climbs above the trees. He's obsessively detailed, stumbles over phrasing. Still Eve nods, encouraging— what? Is the flourishing of friendship really very likely? She feels mute. Has she regressed to a place where she can only utter sounds, trusting chance cries will assume syllabic articulation? Speech, that sensual moving of the air by one person reaching toward another. She notes the Golden Shower tree riffled by a breeze. We say *by,* though breeze and tree are one being.

Much dwelling on the fact that his future wife was mad with longing for him. Does he want to impress upon Eve the fact of his attractiveness? Or is this obsessiveness merely an offshoot of his struggle with English? She wills herself to listen. After all, he's Siva's and Mani's friend, presumably interesting, if only she can find a way to discover this.

In the street two voices, calling back and forth. She focuses on the whorls and inflections of these voices for the pure pleasure of the sounds. Even when two people don't know each other's language, it's the speaker who holds sway—or seems to—while the listener waits. There is, though, something respectful in this waiting, even when the listener's impatient. For the listener is not without power. Eve offers Lallith the little present of a question, so that he may speak to her.

—Did you love her?

Lallith studies the floating dharma blossoms. Love isn't a sanctioned subject of conversation in this country. She has given him opportunity to flirt with what's forbidden.

—Passion for a woman comes to me like a flower blooms, he says. —Then the flower dies. I do not use the word love for this. I love my mother, my sister.

She reminds herself they are next door to a nation where a handsome and very Western looking native woman has just published a book called *Surviving Men*. But suppose he intended to say that when he loves it's forever, that love is properly family love, that he loves his wife because they're married?

Sound of someone climbing the steps: it's Mani, returned.

—I'm driving Vasuhi to preschool. Eve, will you come?

—I'd love to, Eve says. She stands, smiles. Lallith's face is blank. Is he disappointed? Though he may be relieved. It must be toil for him, trying to talk to her.

—Vasuhi! Mani calls.

The little girl appears, eyes sparks, a mischievous smile. Vasuhi makes Eve think of bubbles.

Siva's bees, slumbering in their hive. Eve is careful to skirt the tortoise, amber mound of sonorous silence. She has been sent by Mani to pick curry leaves. Their unassuming appearance, Eve thinks, belies their fury.

She'd met Siva in Kuala Lumpur. He'd presented a paper at a conference on ecology and sustainable development. She'd come to learn: a study vacation, she called it. As a child she'd spent afternoons building bridges for water striders, constructing leafy quarters for cicadas. On to botanical drawing, leading to her lust for tropical forests. Siva, as a boy, had taken to lizards, admiring their tireless knack for the stationary. He'd declared their sunning rocks historic monuments, then tried these warm stones himself, on his back, looking up through lidded eyes.

He'd invited her to meet his family, see his garden, the Center where he'd planted one of every native plant he could get his hands on. This is her second visit. Here are ducks, a resident mongoose. Here is cardamom, good for the brain. Allspice, lackadaisical aphrodisiac. And this one, the sap of this bush—Eve can't remember the name—cleans the blood.

Is that the temple gong? Siva's Center is a sanctuary in a country under siege from foreign investors. At the conference where they'd met, a string of performers had read aloud the names of endangered species. The readers changed, but the sounding of the names continued four days. When the conference ended, the last reader walked out, still intoning names from a printed list.

Her small basket's full. She steps around the tortoise, and suddenly remembers: she'd met Lallith, briefly, the previous year. It was the night before she was leaving. She'd helped Mani serve tea to six men who'd assembled mysteriously with Siva in the living room. Though, of course, their coming was mysterious only to her. Without language you're outside the realm, cast away from the green meanings around you.

She remembers not liking the sound of Lallith's voice, its uninflected drone. It's how he sounds in English too, as though words don't arise spontaneously but are produced repetitively, like piecework. He'd seemed not to notice her. While Mani got the girls ready for bed, Eve slipped away to use the typewriter in Siva's study. Suddenly Lallith had appeared in the doorway.

—Your painting wins a prize! he'd said. —Siva tells me.

The ubiquitous present tense.

—Please, may I see photos.

She hadn't had photos with her. He'd expressed regret. Still, he was eager to invite her to his studio.

—I will carry you to them, he'd said, meaning his oils. Had he smiled then? He'd been eager without trying to mask it, an eagerness that had seemed too blatantly a desire to make a useful connection. But useful in what way? A foreigner is still exotic here, and if the foreigner's a woman, and single, men imagine—what? Asian women were supposed to be devoted, subservient, chaste. It was assumed Western women were promiscuous. People watched too much television, Eve thought.

What he probably wanted was contacts in the world of painting. He'd pushed his bad English at her, his eagerness a pressure. But she was leaving the following day. Oh. His energy sank back. Suddenly she'd felt like an investment not worth making. So, she'd decided, that's the end of it. She'd forgotten his name.

The light is orange, late sun sliding through fire. The girls eat first, then go off to look for fireflies. Eve chops eggplant. Mani browns the bits in oil.

—Lallith talks for a very long time, Eve says. Mani raises her eyebrows.

—These men, always talking! And what good is this oh-so-important talk? Does my husband get up in the dark when Vasuhi has a fever? No. I get up.

—And the next morning you get up on time just the same.

—Exactly. I'm the one who gets the girls ready. Also Siva spends too much money. The money goes like—what do you say?

—Like water, Eve says. —He spends money like water. But Siva's good to you? And to the girls?

—Yes, of course. But his faults, they irritate me so! You said it in the car, about cooking, remember?

Eve remembers. They'd been driving to a party, Siva at the wheel. Siva had asked Eve what dish she most liked cooking.

—Salad, she'd said, laughing. Siva launched into a description of a dish he'd learned to make as a student at Oxford.

—Siva! Eve teased. —I haven't seen you in the kitchen. When will I get to taste this dish?

—Soon, soon, he'd said.

—Really? Eve replied. —I can hardly wait, Siva.

Eve and Mani hadn't tried very hard to suppress their giggling. Now they giggle again.

—Men! Eve says, laughing. —Why do we put up with them?

Mani giggles. —It's we who make the world go, with our breasts full of milk!

She carries a platter of eggplant into the dining room.

—Go, will you. Call those men to come to us so we can feed them.

Eve steps through the arch into dusklight. Siva holds a folded newspaper. Which language are they speaking, Siva's or Lallith's? Both?

—You've come to join us? Siva says.

Eve shakes her head. —The food's ready.

Lallith stands. He'd come back at the end of the day— from what? Negotiating with politicos? Devising strategy for encouraging peace talks? They move toward the dining room.

—This shooting! Siva says. He lays the folded paper on the sideboard. The four of them at the table form two axes. Eve opposite Mani, the female coordinate. —Both of these dopes were members of Parliament. Elected to serve the people! And one simply guns down the other!

Eve has read the English language papers. The murderer asked permission to keep his gold ring and its precious stone with him in the cell. He wanted the stone's protection. The middle class still consults oracles. Marriages are subject to both parties' horoscopes.

—He wore a bulletproof vest, Mani says.

—Surely his party's cachet will suffer? Eve asks.

—Yes, Lallith says. —And before this shooting, already his party has many bad deeds.

—That party is in trouble, Siva says. He'd been a student revolutionary, with the other young men back from Moscow, from Cuba, from Berkeley, Siva from Oxford. They would bring things right; they would act in solidarity. But things got out of hand. Some had opted for blood. Siva had drawn a line: he hadn't killed anyone.

—Their people are all Marxists from the Middle Ages! They want to let things get really bad, then they think the revolution will have to come. In the meantime they cut down our precious forests, and if the catchments don't fill, it doesn't occur to them to develop solar power.

—You're not factoring in the West, Eve says. —The World Bank insisting on privatization. The foreign-owned factories are here for cheap labor. That's why your government refuses striking workers' demands.

—Of course, Siva says. —But believe me, people here are not educated. They don't know who Fritjof Capra is. They don't know quantum physics. They don't care about saving our native plants.

—We are crude, Lallith says.

Will she ever see him smile? She thinks of the Keedarong downstairs in the courtyard, a dwarf variety from

Sumatra. The Keedarong, its blossom the largest of any inflorescence. The flower, when it blooms once a year, is taller than a man. Bless me, Eve thinks, watching Lallith. Bloom, friend, while I'm here.

—Here, only killing gets attention, Lallith says.

—And now we have this power shortage, Mani adds.

Siva slams down his fist.

—The government deliberately drained the catchments so the insurgents couldn't blow them up! That's why we have this shortage!

Mani catches Eve's eye. They smile. Outside in the dark the foliage is speaking in tongues.

Suma, the eldest girl, leans over her workbook. Morning.

—Father, she says in English. —Please buy a new pen. This one is stopped writing.

—Has stopped writing, Siva says.

On the verandah the four drink milk tea. Screech and swoop of parrots. Another bird, its song like an oboe. Crows, harsh shards flung down on the roof. Eve thinks of the Lakota, how they say the robin's call is a long sentence. *Those are cod entrails down there on the bank, my brother-in-law tells me to eat them.* Now the elders say the robin's sentence is degenerating. There are parts left out. The robin has begun to sound like a foreigner, uncertain, just beginning to learn the lingo.

Vasuhi climbs into Mani's lap. She lifts a handful of rice, opens her hand, watches the grains fall onto Mani's plate.

—If you play with your rice like that, you can't go to America, Siva says. —The authorities won't give you a visa.

The temple gong.

—School! Vasuhi says.

Mani ties Vasuhi's sash. —Get your thermos.

Eve and Lallith follow Mani and the girls down and head for the bus stand. The day is scaldingly bright. Eve opens her umbrella against the sun. They weave through the throng, passing the temple grounds. Pilgrims stand inside the gate in a mass, waiting for the monk to appear. In this light the dagoba's whiteness is unanswerable.

When the bus arrives, Lallith insists on paying Eve's fare. They have to stand, hold onto the bar. Their bodies sway. Suddenly Eve remembers Siva's warning. Once, in a passion—Siva's phrase—Lallith had been about to leave his wife. Siva had counseled him, convinced him to stay in the marriage.

—He's hotheaded, Siva told Eve. —He could take a liking to you. If you're alone with him, he might seize you in a passion, kiss you.

He hadn't. Now, on this swaying bus, Lallith seems without any passion whatsoever. Though his silence probably means he's struggling to construct a sentence. The bus passes a restaurant she remembers. She asks if he's been there. He nods.

—Do you want to eat there now? he asks.

She shakes her head. —Not now.

Would she want to eat with him, the two of them alone? A man and woman sharing food has implications, but she's hazy about exactly what the implications are. She'll ask Mani. When two women descend, she and Lallith take their seats. She watches Lallith's mouth. He is plotting a sentence in his mind, sprucing it up, getting ready to deploy it.

—I will accompany you to the bank, he says. —I can show you the way.

Does he imagine she couldn't find her way alone? Does he believe women need men to mediate a world whose complexity is beyond them? She would like to shake him off. As soon as they get off this bus, she'll say good-bye, wave, walk away—but of course she won't. That would be rude.

—It's kind of you, Eve says. —But there's no need to come with me. I know how to find the bank. And you have an appointment.

—I will come with you, he says. —Then I go to my appointment.

He tells her again how at one point the insurgents wanted to murder him.

—Why did they want to kill you?

She dislikes the way being around him makes her turn up the volume without meaning to, as though the problem is making him hear. He explains that when he was a student, someone was—what? Jealous? This someone told the rebel leader Lallith was a spy for the army. The story convolutes. Eve misses words here and there. Lallith mispronounces others, throwing her off. Suddenly the whole enterprise of their being together seems overwhelming: tiresome his struggle to speak, tiresome her failure to understand. Add in this heat, and irritation becomes exhaustion. She closes her eyes, rests in darkness.

When she opens her eyes, Lallith is looking at her.

—Can you understand me? he asks.

—Sometimes. Not all the time.

He turns up his hands, that gesture of despair. In this pause, before he speaks, finally, the sentence that will turn the little key inside her, opening her to whatever he wants, she hesitates: has she hurt him by admitting that his English is difficult to understand? The two of them are heat, mute. They might as well have turned into foliage. Eve looks at her hands. The whorls of the fingertips and toes are evidence of the wind inside you, the breath with which you speak. And two little winds are there in each ear. These are the winds that help you hear.

He turns to her his liquid eyes, those eyes of anthracite, jet, sable.

—In regard to your language, he says—I'm a hunter-gatherer.

It's as though the first upright creature has spoken the first articulate sentence. O nimble tongue! Orphic utterance! This sentence may be a fluke. He may have stumbled unwittingly into momentary eloquence. Or it might be a sentence he's lifted from a novel, saving it for just such a situation. Even in his own tongue he may be without nuance, his speech brute inarticulate. But Eve doesn't care. She's in love with his sentence. Her laugh resembles the bright spilling of water.

—Come with me to the bank, she says. —Please. Then, if you have time, we'll eat something together. Would you like that?

There it is, his smile.

It's her laugh, she understands, that has made this smile possible. Just as his whimsical remark unlocked her laughter. One thing kisses the thing next to it, nudging the next stammering syllable into being. His sentence is the utterance she's been waiting for, the way pilgrims wait for the monk to appear, wait for his voice to ignite the air.

THE THING
AROUND THEM

1

It was because of the boy dragged behind the jeep that Vasuki gave Nadesan the money to buy the ticket. When she went to her brother with the bills tucked into her sari, she did not speak the language of the master countries, nor did she know anyone who had traveled there. She was aware that at some point the island had been occupied by foreign powers, but she was not sure which powers, or when. That the Portuguese had stayed until driven out by the Dutch; that the Dutch were driven out by the British; that the British had granted the island its independence when the Crown's hand had been forced by its other colonies—these were facts she had never been told by anyone. Or if she had been told these things by a teacher, or heard them referred to by a politician campaigning for a seat in Parliament, they were not facts which had seemed important. What she knew about the master countries was that there was abundance in such degree that even the few poor were well off. People lived together peacefully and moved about the streets of the cities and the roads between towns without fear. She'd watched her son's face that same afternoon, how it had become lit when she gave him grain to feed the chickens. She'd taken pleasure in seeing Poniah's pleasure, and then she had thought of the boy behind the jeep.

Vasuki had seen this boy on the school playground, a cricket bat in hand. Afterward, at the funeral, Vasuki approached the boy's mother, touched her papery hand. It had become clear to Vasuki who she herself was: she was Mannika's mother, Poniah's mother. She had a girl, she had a boy, and her boy would grow to the same age as the boy behind the jeep.

He had shy eyes and a smile like the flash of a parrot bursting from banana leaves. But the soldiers insisted this boy spied for the insurgents. She imagined the scene as a kind of haze, its outline vibratory in the way that memories of childhood shimmer and have no edge. The boy's mother had had to watch the soldiers throw her son down. They'd tied one foot to the back fender of the jeep. One foot, tied at the ankle. Then they had climbed into the jeep and driven off, shouting in that language no one could understand.

When Vasuki thought of her childhood, she remembered herself inside a shimmering sphere, a globe of green air. Her body was itself a small globe, tenuous and full and open, merging with air, foliage, the waters of the lagoon, and the other bodies moving with her through the green light. Her parents had rocked her the way a boat is rocked by water, and it had been as though the three of them and all that surrounded them were the body of a single animal, sliding from the bank into the water, moving with the lagoon's lapping, which moved with the sea and the currents of the air.

Vasuki and Sri had run back and forth with their brothers in that green light. Nadesan was the second son. He was their clown, miming the ridiculous in adults. Sometimes he mimed Vasuki, her dreaminess and awe. Then she threw handfuls of sand at him. He ran, ducking, protesting. He would cover his head with his hands in mock distress, until she too was laughing.

She loved Nadesan for his merriment. With Sinniah, the eldest, she felt like his cherished child. She heard him shout her name: Vasuki! The timbre of his voice made it sound as if her name were made of gold. He took charge, planning expeditions to the flame trees' shade, instructing them to pack food in banana leaves, bring their thermoses. When Vasuki and Sri quarreled, he calmed them. "Don't pull your sister's hair. Be nice to each other." He taught them the names of birds, the properties of the alari. They could gather the yellow blossoms, but they should never touch the poisonous seeds.

Vasuki observed Sinniah leaning over his books in an ardor of concentration. He would take care of them all, he said, when their parents were old. "I'll find handsome husbands for you both," he told his sisters. "I'll work to make your dowries big."

In school there were clear rules, a single language. Vasuki imagined it was the universal language spoken by people everywhere, and she went on imagining this until the army set up headquarters in the town. The army had come to protect people from the insurgents. Though the soldiers spoke a language no one could understand, the mayor said they were friendly. Neither Vasuki's mother nor father had actually seen the soldiers, though Sinniah had looked into the back of a lorry turning a corner. It held many men standing close, in dark green uniforms, each with his own rifle. Nadesan had run with his friends to the cricket field, watched the soldiers marching in formation. Or was this an exercise he'd seen on the TV at the electronics shop? Nadesan's tales they didn't always believe. Still, when he mimed the soldiers' drill—their abrupt, mechanical movements—even their mother and father laughed.

Evenings then were a span of light in which the air softened, and blue sank toward black. Their father pulled Sri onto his lap, kissed her cheek. Sri laughed with the pleasure of being at the center of his attentive affection. The smell of limes drifted in the heated dampness. Then there were soldiers—how many?—bunched in the doorway.

One of the soldiers spoke to their father in that other language. He gestured for their father to follow. Their father moved Sri from his lap and stood. Vasuki understood that somehow he had made these men angry. She felt ashamed. Her father must have done something shameful. But she was also afraid for him. It was as though something foreign had entered the compound, something dark and shifting that not even the soldiers could see. She tried to find its shape in the air, but the soldiers had burst through the green shimmering, ripping it. The soldier who'd spoken spat out an order. Two others had moved forward, taken hold of their father and swept him through the doorway, down the path to the jeep.

To have a person snatched away as though a slit had been cut in the green air and he had been pulled through! That same night two others who cut timber with Vasuki's father were also arrested. No insurgents had appeared where they were cutting, and none of them had imagined that working in the forest where the insurgents were said to roam might cast suspicion on them. It was true that the insurgents, who had first built their camps in the north, had later built camps here, but these were inland, away from the town. They collected taxes, but after all they had to. They were fighting for Eelam, that heaven on earth. The fighters visited schools in the towns and surrounding villages, recruiting young boys. Sometimes they wanted your firewood or one of your bags of rice, but usually they paid. Once, three young men in spotted uniforms had come, asking for petrol. When Vasuki's mother said they had none, the three had gone on.

"Who were they, in those funny clothes?" Vasuki had asked.

"Just some men needing petrol," her mother said. "Bring me a bucket of water from the well."

Each time Vasuki's mother and the other wives inquired at the army camp, the sergeant was courteous. He spoke their language, and he invited them to sit down. He listened while they repeated their petitions. Then he said he was very sorry to tell them the army knew nothing about the whereabouts of their husbands. Still, he assured them, the army cared for their welfare. Inquiries would be made.

Vasuki's mother had heard there were men in the north who, like her husband, had been taken away. Some had returned and some had not. But she had not credited these rumors. Even when her husband was taken, she continued to believe he was not one of those who would not be released. There had been some mistake, and she believed the sergeant would find it. While she waited, the army set up more camps south of the town.

Then the police arrested six fishermen. The next day four were released. The other two they gave to the army for questioning. When her husband's cousin was arrested in a northern town, Vasuki's mother did not tell her children. She told them this cousin had gone to the capital to take a plane to the Middle East where he had found work. Vasuki listened. Her mother did not seem especially pleased by this news, but since her father had been arrested, a certain anxiousness had become the horizon note in her mother's being.

One afternoon when her mother had gone to the sergeant's office, Vasuki came home from school and began to eat a bowl of pittu. Her mother came through the gate. She picked an alari blossom, entered and placed it on the table. Slanted sunlight fell across the flower. Her mother's face was as though fallen in.

"What is it?" Vasuki said. "Did someone hit you?"

"No," her mother said. Vasuki thought of the Catholic priest who, though her family was not Catholic, had volunteered to intercede for them with the sergeant. He had used an expression Vasuki had not heard before: the disappeared.

Through the doorway Vasuki could see the lagoon, a single boat, bobbing. Though she could see nothing out of the ordinary, it seemed that this boat which sat innocently on the water was in danger. Something could rip the boat from the water, and, in a moment, splinter it. When Vasuki turned back, the light had moved. Now the blossom lay in shadow. Her mother's face was an opening into a vast place where anyone might quickly be lost.

2

Vasuki lifted her new son Poniah from the bath and held him above her. Droplets shimmered from his skin. Her daughter Mannika sat in the tin tub of water and chattered. Vasuki could hear the clink of pans, her mother moving about the kitchen. Two Golden Shower trees across the road floated in yellow haze, and the flame trees in back sent up their red fires. The lagoon at midday burned too fiercely to look at. It would have been like looking into the sun.

Vasuki seldom thought of her father. This was the house where her father had lived with them, even her mother rarely spoke of him. The army had pulled out, moving its troops north. Then Raj. He was tall. Height singled him out. People turned their bodies toward him. Because he inspired trust, he'd been asked to join the citizens' committee. Though he left for the pharmacy each morning, the effect of his height lingered in the compound. He was there, or nearby. He was going, or coming. The sun climbed its arc, leveled, slid down the sky. At twilight he returned. Vasuki stood in the doorway. She was the color red, its heated pulse. When Mannika was born, Vasuki assumed the mother's place in the ancestral house. Now the family had a man to tend its flame, and Raj was the priest, holding aloft the burning camphor, approaching the inner room of the temple. At the center stood Vasuki, the flaming mouth.

Now the army had appeared again. Soldiers had set up camp. They'd set up checkpoints with bunkers at either end of the bridge leading into the town. When women went to the market, the soldiers made them line up, show their identification cards, open their bags.

The soldiers had been sent to protect the people from the fighters, but this was the insurgent's home turf, and they spoke the language, and the soldiers didn't. You could see how nervous the soldiers were. At night a few insurgents might enter the town to get food, or petrol. Once in a while one of them threw a grenade into an army bunker. Among the civilians the soldiers were supposed to protect some were bound to sympathize with the fighters. The soldiers were especially suspicious of young men. Young men might be fighters out of uniform, come into the town to buy food. Even if they weren't, they might help the fighters get petrol or repair a vehicle.

Sometimes the soldiers let the young man go the next morning. Sometimes they kept him a few days, then transferred him to the civil prison. It was thought important that the young man's family go to the army camp as quickly after an arrest as possible. Getting there quickly might make a difference. Once a father and two uncles had gone immediately, taking a lawyer with them, and the son had been released. People tried to find someone of stature to speak for them. They offered the sergeant what money they had.

One young man who'd been kept almost a year had come back. His story was not a good one. Things had been done to him, things with electricity. Things with water. And yet the moon rose and set, moving the ocean's ablutions. The green curtain rippled when a breeze blew over the lagoon. Birds sang out their vibratory calls before dawn, urging the sun onto its arc. The air tasted sweet. Light laid on its hands.

Poniah made the soft sounds of a baby. Vasuki kissed him on both cheeks, blew air against the skin of his belly. His arms waved. He reminded her of a fat insect turned onto its back. Each morning she watched Raj ride toward the bridge on his bicycle, heading for the pharmacy his family owned. She'd heard Nadesan and Sinniah leave early. For three weeks they'd worked a construction job Raj had helped them get by speaking to the foreman. The pay was good, and they gave their wages for household expenses. Sinniah wanted to go to University, but hadn't qualified. Today he was excused from work to take the entrance exam again. She'd recognized Nadesan's voice wishing Sinniah good luck.

STORIES BY MARILYN KRYSL

She kissed Mannika's shoulder, then eased the dress over her daughter's head. While Mannika ate, Vasuki fed Poniah bites of milkrice. Her mother went into the yard to take down laundry. Mannika examined her plastic wristwatch, playing at telling time. Now Poniah closed his lips against the bite she offered. He blew air through pursed lips and arched his back. He wanted down.

Her mother stood beside the gate, speaking to someone. Vasuki recognized Nadesan's voice. Then her mother's cry. Her mother lurched across the sand, arms around a sheaf of clothes.

"Sinniah!" Their mother sank to her knees, threw herself over the heap of laundry. "Get Raj to come with us. Vasuki! Go ask him!"

Nadesan knelt beside his mother. "I'll go for Raj," he said. He looked at Vasuki. "Four soldiers were shot. In a jeep, not far from the University, where the coconut trees are. The army closed the campus. They rounded up the men students—seventy of them. Seventy, Vasuki. They made them stand against a wall. Then they took them away in lorries."

"They'll let some of them go," their mother said. "There's no reason to keep Sinniah. He's not a student."

"When has reason mattered?" Nadesan said. "Four soldiers were shot."

Poniah had been wiggling in his chair. Now he sat, watching them, sensing urgency. The color of his eyes reminded Vasuki of the polished stones along the lagoon's edge, if these stones were to come alive.

Poniah learned to walk. Mornings, he toddled after his father, stood at the gate and watched him wheel away. He picked alari flowers and took them to Mannika. He liked Mannika to sing to him. They played in the sand, molding mounds and basins. Sometimes Sri brought her baby girl and sat in the shade with the children while Vasuki took their mother to the market.

In midday heat Poniah fell asleep against Vasuki's breast. Above the cadjun fence she could see the lagoon. The water seemed a thing alive, part of the sea's body that had flowed inland, shimmering like thousands of floating coins. People had got together a citizens' committee. This committee kept records of those who were arrested and passed this information to the member of Parliament from their district. Sinniah hadn't been released. Nor did the army admit to having taken him.

At night they heard firing in the distance. Biking home, Raj saw the faint flash of mortars. The papers reported good things and bad things. A new five-star hotel had opened in the capital. Nine village boys were picked up by soldiers, kept for a day, then delivered to the civil prison. There was a new TV program in which the women looked like women from the master countries. Nineteen boys were lured away by videos the fighters had shown at the high school. A new fertilizer plant opened in a city to the south which would employ three thousand people. The fighters blew up two oil storage tanks on the outskirts of the capital, the police rounded up young men for questioning, and ten days later twenty-three bodies were found floating in a lake twenty miles away. The young men's hands had been tied behind their backs.

People talked about the thing around them—how you couldn't see how big it might be, how you couldn't tell when it would come. Even the son of the barrister, on the train to the capital, had been caught in the insurgents'

STORIES BY MARILYN KRYSL

ambush. The doctor's daughter walked partway home from school with her friends, waved to them, went on alone. The girls had followed this pattern every day. One day this daughter hadn't come home.

A lime green parrot squawked and flew across the compound. Vasuki carried Poniah inside, lay besided him on the mat. No one said much about the fighters. Their struggle was for the people, but though they usually paid for what they took, their taxes were in addition to the government's taxes. The sons of some fishermen and shopkeepers had joined them. Some girls had joined too. Some of these children had been killed in scrimmages with the army. One girl from the town who'd joined and then died in a battle with the soldiers was hailed by the insurgents as a martyr hero. Raj and Vasuki had seen her photograph tacked to a lamp post.

There were also boys in the town who'd trained with the fighters, then become disillusioned. Once they deserted, they wanted to go abroad. Some went from house to house, demanding money. They threatened to identify a son or daughter to the army as a supporter of the fighters. When one of them agreed to act as an informer, the soldiers took him to the check point beside the bridge. They covered his head with a black hood. He watched the people passing the checkpoint. The ones he pointed to were taken away.

Vasuki turned onto her side. She liked to look at Poniah while he slept. His breath was sweet. She had learned that most people on the island spoke the army's language. It was the language of the group from which the Prime Minister and most members of Parliament had been elected. It was not her language, but it hadn't mattered. There was a member of Parliament from her district, and there were TV programs in her language. Just last week a policeman from the group whose language Vasuki spoke and a policewoman from the larger group had celebrated their wedding at a local hotel.

Some people also spoke the language of the master countries. Raj had told Vasuki that when the British left, the larger group on the island had dominated Parliament. They'd declared their language the official language. Suddenly people who spoke Vasuki's language couldn't do business, couldn't get a job. In the next generation the two groups had managed to renegotiate the issue of language. For a while both languages on the island and the master language were taught in schools. Then the government began to promote the idea that native languages were superior, and the master language was dropped from the curriculum. Lately it had been reinstated. Mannika was learning songs in this language.

Vasuki had heard there was war in the master countries too, small bits of fighting that took place in fragments: groups of boys in gangs, policemen attacking a man with dark skin, a crowd burning shops owned by Koreans. And war within families: sons killing a father, a father raping a daughter, a husband killing his adulterous wife. She thought these stories were probably exaggerated. Anyway, those things were not war. Besides, people said that most of those who went there became wealthy. It would be to their son's advantage, she told Raj, if he could learn the language of the larger group and a bit of the master language too.

On the afternoon Raj was stopped on the bridge, Mannika had come out of school carrying the drawing she'd made of an umbrella. Though she was seven and could walk to school by herself, Vasuki had begun to accompany her. She left Poniah at Sri's house and picked him up on the way back. There was wind that day, and Vasuki put her arm around Mannika to shield her. Mannika explained how first she'd chosen red for the umbrella, then blue, then changed her mind a third time to yellow. Finally she'd decided to make each panel of the umbrella a different color. When she'd done that, there were still colors she hadn't used. So many colors, and they all deserved to be seen. What was one to do?

Vasuki had thought ahead to Raj's arrival. She would repeat Mannika's story. He would be amused. When they'd picked up Poniah, Vasuki carried him, trying to protect him from the wind's whipping. Mannika complained that she too needed to be carried. At their gate the wind had blown down a scatter of alari blossoms. Vasuki brought the children inside to play.

Later the wind stopped. The quiet seemed pristine. Like a god stepping down, it announced itself. Then Nadesan came through the gate, calling her, her name and her husband's name in his mouth. It was not until after she and Nadesan had left the sergeant's office that she remembered a thing she'd noticed that afternoon. While Mannika and Poniah played on the floor, wind had roughed up the lagoon's surface. The ripples had seemed as though beaten with a whip, as though the wind were flaying a skin.

For the second year the rains had not come. People had to carry water from the few wells in the town deep enough to reach what was left. Drought leached color from leaves. The sky was dun. Sometimes the wind picked up a sheet of sand and blew it against the houses.

Inside herself Vasuki constructed a pyre like the one on which the family would have cremated Raj's body. She would not be like those other women, helplessly waiting. She would not wait. She would not hope. She was the mother. She stood up inside that space Raj had attended. She would become even more fiercely the mother.

She lit the pyre. The sticks caught. Flame after flame rose up in conflagration. She imagined this heat destroying all hurt, redeeming Raj from the pain he had surely suffered. Each time she felt herself beginning to long for him, she went back to the pyre and stood there. She fed the flame sticks. She brought it food. She gave it flowers. She stood watch over this burning.

Vasuki was preparing to take the children with her for water. When Pohiah saw Nadesan at the gate, he came running. His uncle picked Poniah up and lifted him high.

"You are a bird!" Nadesan said. "Now you will fly!"

Poniah laughed and wriggled. Nadesan set him down and he ran back to Mannika. She took him by the hand and drew him toward the gate. She was at the top of her class. At home she flitted from one part of the house to another, and in these quick movements she seemed to be sparkling. She liked teaching Poniah songs, and she sat him on her lap and read to him in the master language. He gazed in the distance, eagerly and with a small frown, imagining the events Mannika described.

"Give me those two jars," Nadesan said. "I'll walk with you to the queue." The four of them stepped into the lane, and the children ran ahead.

"You see how quickly she's learning," Vasuki said. "Poniah too."

"Smart kids," Nadsan said. "But is this language fad really for the best?"

Nadesan had been approached with marriage proposals from four families. There were fewer young men now, and more women had to go without husbands. Nadesan was handsome, and his mischievousness had matured into an attractive cheerfulness. He chose a girl whose family was cashew growers. Now that he was married and his wife pregnant, he liked to instruct, to make pronouncements.

"In one of those places you're so crazy about, things aren't so good for people like us," he said. "Last week some Turks there got beaten up."

Vasuki swung the water jar impatiently. "There may have been some incident or other, but everyone knows people there are rich."

"The Turks were sleeping, and their hostel got set on fire by a crowd. People watched the fire raise up, and they cheered. Can you imagine?"

"Mannika! Don't get so far ahead!" Vasuki called.

"Then the Turks who ran out of the burning building were caught and beaten."

Poniah fell back and skipped beside his uncle. Mannika took her mother's free hand.

"People there want to adopt foreign children," Vasuki said, "so why would they beat up foreigners? While here the army bans fishing because those fighters threw grenades over the fence near the brigadier's headquarters."

There was not much fish in the market, and vegetables were expensive. You couldn't get widow's compensation without a death certificate, and you couldn't get a death certificate for a person unless you could prove they had died. The army sergeant continued to insist that the army did not have Raj in custody, nor did they know of his whereabouts.

When Nadesan moved into his wife's ancestral house, he'd continued to give Vasuki money. Raj's younger brother took over the pharmacy, and he was able to give Vasuki a little each week. Raj had put away money against emergencies, and now Vasuki added this to his brother's gifts and the money from Nadesan.

"Anyone there can become a doctor or scientist or the head of a manufacturing firm," she said. "They have washing machines and vacuum cleaners. Everyone has a VCR and a car."

"Maybe," Nadesan said. "Anyway, we're not going there. Except for Poniah." He picked up Poniah again and flew him above their heads. "Poniah will fly through the air right out of the country!"

"I'm going to fly!" Poniah said. He laughed.

Nadesan was proud in that strutting way of a rooster. But he'd said it, spontaneously, as though it were true: Poniah, flying out of the country. The day before, Vasuki had stood in the queue for water. The women waiting talked. America had sent Green Berets to help train the soldiers. The generals had expected that with the Americans would come better, more expensive equipment which would enable them to rout the insurgents. Young men who had previously shunned the army's ranks signed up. They wanted to be near these foreign soldiers who wore their tall, powerful bodies like uniforms and looked as though nothing could stand against them.

Soon after the Green Berets arrived, the army announced the north had been "cleared." This freed troops for the east. Suddenly there were many more soldiers in the town. When their lorries weren't enough, they commandeered public buses. One woman in the queue said she'd set off to attend a funeral but there had been no bus.

Many of the soldiers were nervous new recruits. And the fighters were known to have suicide squads. A village woman's bag of vegetables might hide a bomb. Or one of the army lorries might hit a mine. One way or another, the women agreed, it was only a matter of time before more soldiers or even a brigadier got killed. Then there would be a very bad incident. Young men would be rounded up, or the soldiers might set a village afire, or arrest fishermen because their work in the sun made their skins very dark, like the skins of the fighters who lived in the open.

"The best thing," one of the women said, "would be if a big bomb came and killed all of us at once."

She thought of Nadesan's joking pronouncement: Poniah flying. She imagined her son as a cherub, with little wings. Nadesan turned to his sister. He would become a father. Ensconced in this dispensation, he spoke with confidence.

"It may be that people there have cars," he said, "but things are going to get better here. You'll see."

Nadesan's head was filled with dreams, Vasuki thought, all because his wife had a big belly. Vasuki went regularly to the temple to pray for her children's safety. She had taken a vow, asked the goddess to protect them. To perform the vow, she had walked the fire with the other women, carrying Poniah in her arms.

Still, at times, a searing fear shot through her. A slit in the air—you couldn't see it, but suddenly someone who'd been right beside you was pulled out. Sons more than daughters. Though more and more it seemed what was around them might devour a daughter as easily as a son. The soldiers picked up girls at random, kept them a few days, dropped them by the side of the road. Some lay in the ditch and did not move. Others managed to walk back to their houses. One lay in bed two months, then died. Some came back to their parents' houses, then swallowed the poisonous seeds of the alari.

3

Something happened that had never happened because no soldier or general had thought of it. It began when fighters attacked an army camp near the town, killed fifty-two soldiers and set three tents on fire. Soldiers shot farmers in their fields. They burned houses. In the town no queues were formed. No buses ran. Shops closed. People went into their houses and shut the doors.

A day and a night passed. Then the news came. Soldiers had cut the coconut trees. They said it was to use the trunks for bunkers, but they'd cut every tree. Orchard after orchard, all the way back to that first generation fell in this cutting. Even the orchards which belonged to the Catholic priests were cut without a single piece of paper granting dispensation.

Vasuki left the children with Sri and went to where the orchards had been. It felt as though angry speech had shot out across the air, cursing whatever lovely thing was in its path. The stumps were white, shocking. You didn't want to walk there. There was too much sadness in that place.

At the end of the third day of the army's assault, Nadesan's wife went into labor. The labor went on longer than it should have. When the midwife pulled the baby out, the little boy was dead.

That was the day soldiers tied the boy's foot to the bumper of their jeep. Afterward the jeep had come back. The driver had halted on the main street. The boy's mother hurried to meet it, then stood a little away, watching one of the soldiers step down. If he noticed her, he paid no attention. He'd taken a knife from his belt and cut the rope.

The next day Vasuki gave Nadesan the money. She asked him to buy the ticket. He agreed. The baby's death had sealed off his cheerfulness. Afterward she took the children to the lagoon. Poniah squatted and set his paper boat onto the swaying water. He watched the boat rocking on the waves and sang one of the songs Mannika had taught him. He reminded Vasuki of one of the tiny chittering frogs that appeared in the mud after a rain.

"Look!" he said. Five gulls wheeled over the water.

"You're going to fly like one of those gulls," Vasuki said. She explained he would travel in a very big airplane to a new country where there were no soldiers. On the plane there would be a kind auntie who would give him sweets and a toy airplane to play with while the big plane flew through the sky.

The gulls flew toward the sea. She explained that she and Mannika would come a little later. Mannika frowned. Would Sri and their cousins come too? Their uncle Nadesan? Their grandmother? Vasuki nodded.

"Poniah's too little to go alone," Mannika said. "I should go with him."

"You would leave your mother alone?" Vasuki teased.

"Of course not," Mannika said. "We would send for you as soon as we got there."

The neighbor's bitch, a small terrier, had come in heat. Her suitors came, baying in the moonlight, sprinting up and down the fence. Vasuki got up, filled a bucket with the bad well water and threw it on them. In the ensuing quiet she slept without dreams. She woke early and went through the gate into the lane. To the west the full moon stood just above the horizon. To the east the sun was appearing over the water. She stood exactly between these poles. Encompassed by the timed motion of these bodies, she felt her decision confirmed.

That morning she got a small suitcase ready. In it she put new clothes, small toys. A statue of the goddess. She'd brought the book Mannika was reading to Poniah. She pictured Poniah stepping down from the plane, holding his book. There below, the kind parents, ready to love him, the mother bending over, taking his miniature body into her arms. His mother would be blond. Vasuki imagined the little ways in which this woman would cherish his perfect body. And the father, a tall man, like one of those Green Berets, would be kind. She imagined his approval, his head nodding. He would be proud of this good son.

Green parrots squawked and dove in and out of the banana leaves. The flame trees put forth their fiery petals. When she'd finished her morning chores, she took Poniah to the lagoon. Two butterflies near a margosa swooped in elliptical arcs around each other. A fisherman repairing his boat agreed to give Poniah a ride. They stayed close to shore, and when the fisherman steered the boat in, Poniah climbed out, splashing and smiling.

"Has Mannika been in a boat?" he said. "I don't think so."

At dusk Vasuki let him feed the chickens. They clucked excitedly, running wherever his arm flung the grain. The moon rose over the lagoon. Mannika helped Poniah finish filling the suitcase. He put in a toy truck and a small doll Mannika had given him. Then he brought his favorite sheet from the clothesline.

"It has dried in the moonlight," he announced. He laid the sheet across the doll. Then he ran outside, plucked three alari blossoms and laid them on top.

Earth and air conspired in the darkness, and sweet rain fell in abundance. The Golden Shower trees across the lane and the flame trees in back were drunk with it. Tiny birds perched, ruffling their feathers. Rain dripped from their tails. The sand was pounded, washed clean.

Vasuki lay beside Poniah. When the alarm woke her, rain had ceased. The moon was just going down. She woke Poniah, bathed and dressed him. While Poniah ate, Nadesan arrived, hearty and joking. He would take Poniah to the capital. He'd arranged for another passenger, a distant cousin of his wife's, to look out for Poniah on the flight. He admired his nephew's suitcase. He tapped Poniah on the shoulder and winked.

"You and I are going off to adventure," he said. "The others are not brave enough, and so must stay here where nothing happens."

Mannika still slept, and Poniah went to her and kissed her cheek. He walked with his mother and uncle to the gate. Vasuki kissed him, then stood back. She watched Poniah take his uncle's hand. They stepped through the gate. Poniah turned and waved. She stood in the lane until they turned the corner.

She walked to the house through the cries of parrots. Each morning she heard their raucous calls, like bolts of color shot through the highest branches. This morning each cry sounded like the glint of a blade.

Mannika was gay, getting dressed. She chattered about what Poniah might be doing at that moment. On the walk to school she made up a list of things she and her mother would do together. A lark swooped down before them, its glide a soft whistle, then turned its trajectory up and away. Vasuki was relieved that Mannika didn't seem to miss Poniah too much, at least not yet. The lilt of excitement in Mannika's good-bye seemed to Vasuki a new language the universe was just now creating, language she was barely beginning to hear.

She walked home through the pattern of light and shade spread on the sand. In the compound a yellow bird flitted down to peck grain the chickens missed. It was necessary to boil more drinking water. She wept, and the heat built its esplanade across the day. Geckos slid off into shade. She sat to drink a glass of water. The heat felt like a familiar body, someone she slept next to, and at the same time strange. It was as though a strange new color had been loosed into the world. She could not decide whether this color was beautiful.

A haze of yellow butterflies fluttered above the alari, and on the fence perched two tiny birds, their heads azure. Usually the lane was empty. Five soldiers came striding toward her. Vasuki stepped aside to let them pass. Soldiers did not come here. They stayed on the other side of the bridge. She walked to where the lane met the main road. Now there were many soldiers, spreading out from lorries. Four and five at a time were going door to door, knocking, shouting for the occupants. In one doorway a young man appeared in his sarong, his eyes darting from face to face.

What had happened to make the soldiers come here? Must have been something bigger than a mine. There was the smell of someone's cooking fire. Or was it a cooking fire kicked apart by a soldier? Lucky that Nadesan had gone to the capital, lucky that Sri's husband wouldn't have come home yet. The lagoon water was smooth and perfect as a mirror. She tried to become still, swaying only a little, like water. How slow and soft the air around her, how nervously she was rushing through it.

Then the school was before her, two hibiscus at the gate, their flowers hot orange. The playground was deserted. The principal, a stately woman who always wore sari, let Vasuki in.

"What's happened?" Vasuki asked. Other mothers were gathered just inside the entrance. The principal shook her head.

"Who can say? Best to wait here until the soldiers go back across the bridge. We'll wait together."

Mannika ran to her mother, waving a piece of paper.

"This is our house, at night. You can't see us, because you and Daddy and I and Poniah are sleeping, but here are the trees, and I've put in a moon."

"Soldiers!" a boy called. Through the open casement she saw them. Seven soldiers had come through the gate. Behind them, one at a time, came more soldiers. They spread out in a line facing the school's entrance. In the quiet the children's white uniforms seemed very bright. Vasuki closed her eyes, let them rest for a moment on blankness. When she opened them, she saw a child tugging his mother's sari. His mother lifted him, and he clutched her waist with his legs.

Vasuki looked at the soldiers' faces. How different each face was—one handsome, the next with pocked skin, one fierce, another bewildered, nervous. They were hardly more than school boys. Beyond them the hibiscus put forth its bright blooms, and Vasuki wanted to call out to ask their names, the names of their parents. But none of the soldiers looked at her. The line kept curving until it circled the school.

"Out!" A soldier shouted. He spoke Vasuki's language. "Everyone out."

The principal stepped forward.

"Don't go," one mother said. "Don't open the door."

The principal shook her head. "I'll talk to them. It may be that they only want the building."

Mannika tugged at Vasuki's skirt. Vasuki spoke the appropriate, calming words, but as soon as she'd spoken, she could not remember what she'd said. She thought how the green globe still held in some places. So many rips, so much tearing, and yet a mango was still perfectly what it was. No matter how many soldiers died, you could take a bath, feel the water's sacral pouring. And children kept coming into the world, running from shade to sunlit sand, their voices calling the way gulls call out from their wheeling.

She was glad. Poniah was on his way to a country where kind and wealthy people wanted foreign children. She'd thought ahead, she'd done the right thing. She'd sent her son out of this country of death to another country where he would be safe.

Mannika's body pressed against her hip. In her hand, the drawing. Such a small hand, a hand that gripped a green crayon, moved it decisively across paper. Vasuki saw her own hand, gathering in Mannika's shoulder. She looked at her own long fingers. This was not a hand that could save anyone. It was good only for brushing away flies, for mixing pittu. For a moment, this hand seemed not her own, but the hand of a stranger. Then it occurred to her that there was a thing this hand might do. If the soldiers let them go home, this hand could do it. She imagined this hand pushing open the gate to their compound. She imagined reaching out to the alari, gathering the alari seeds.

MINE

The phone rings at dawn. It's him, Elena thinks. The captain she met at the hotel pool, in the immense heat, in that northern city. Sometimes the wind there blows and piles the heat in dunes. Sometimes it doesn't blow, and then you wish it would. Monkeys chase each other through the margosa trees, chattering, fighting over fallen fruit. At night they swing down from the branches, clatter across the hotel roof in the dark.

She and the Canadian photographer had worked through the heat without a nap. That rectangle of turquoise water was the only water for miles. She swam leisurely laps, then turned onto her back and looked up. The sky was an absolute—a pure, unnameable color.

Captain Mendis was friendly with the manager. Whenever the war backed off, he dropped by in the late afternoon with a few of his buddies. He was in his thirties like she was, though his men looked younger, some of them scarcely more than boys. They horsed around, splashing each other, diving. Though it was difficult for the captain to actually swim. His left knee had been damaged by a mine fragment.

She imagines him now, before reveille, in the barracks office, boots propped on the desk. Shirt open at the neck.

The window open on stillness. Distance. She picks up the phone.

"Elena."

"You woke me."

"I had to call. I need to talk to you. Tell me: what did you think when I took hold of your arm in the pool? I gripped your wrist. We were at the deep end, remember? I asked you if you liked the color of my skin. Do you like it? Tell me."

Hibiscus blossoms streak the air hot orange. Banana trees ring the compound, their leaves bright fringe above the wall. There are no pastels in this country. Everything is boldly what it is, and she responds boldly. Her body feels lush here, overblown, and besides, moderation isn't her style. She believes in big and beautiful—big dreams, a big, generous heart.

Life has breadth, and she wants hers abundant, filled. The hand-held shower's deliciously cool. She'll check out the strike in the Free Trade Zone, then finish that story for her paper. On the streets of the capital you'd scarcely know there's a war on. Once in a while the guerrillas work some sabotage, such as the bomb set off next to Navy headquarters in which a well-known officer was killed. Or the suicide bombing at a political rally in which the parliamentary candidate and fifty of his supporters died. But these occurrences are rare. Afterward the government imposes a curfew for a week, while the anxiety wears itself out. Then things return to business as usual.

She'd flirted with the captain while late afternoon turned into evening. When the floodlights came on, the two of them swam from the deep end to the shallow. She said good-bye and went up to dress for dinner. When she came down, the desk clerk gave her the captain's note, in which he asked if he might meet her the following day. He would phone.

She and the photographer had tickets for the early train. The captain phoned while they were at breakfast. He maintained a formal propriety, and she gave him her number in the capital. If he came, she'd said, he could give her a call.

He couldn't come, but he'd called. Gone was propriety. Of course, she'd thought. She's known other men who liked the phone. It seems to come with the technology. Now he calls every day, sometimes twice. The problem is that he calls very late or very early. And there are the others who share the apartment, another journalist, the photographer, the French nurse who works for *Medicine San Frontiers*.

The captain's limp was slight, but noticeable. He'd been lucky, she thinks. He hadn't died, or lost a leg. He'd survived, though he can't claim to have earned honor. In the matter of mines there can be no valor. Like the ubiquitous Coca-Cola, they have penetrated the most pristine regions. One survives now not through strength or bravery, but by dumb luck.

Still she wonders: did the fact that he limped inspire her sympathy? Is it failure of sympathy that prompts her to reject the photographer's advances? Or those of the handsome journalist who writes for one of the Tamil papers? Or the persistent attaché from the Dutch embassy? The dashing professor of Sinhalese history?

Today she's back at the apartment by noon, finishes the story by six, dines out with the photographer, returns to the apartment. Perhaps after all the timing of the captain's calls is a convenience. She is free to work through the day, to come and go as she pleases. Then, at ten or eleven, he phones.

She imagines him now, in the heat, on that plain at the edge of the jungle, miles from the city. There are no videos, no magazines, no music, nothing but the heat, ticking off arrivals and departures of the endless seconds. The eye, gazing unrelieved at that expanse, closes. Conversation is without modulation, the idle talk of men confined to quarters.

Still, when the phone rings at midnight, she protests.

"You've got to stop calling so late. It disturbs the others." Her role, in their scenario, to invoke propriety; his role to confess that the extremity of his need compels him to violate it.

"You know I have to talk to you," he says. "Tell me, when I gripped your wrist, I wanted to kiss you. I wanted to put my tongue in your mouth. Did you want to feel my tongue push in? Elena? Tell me."

It's five when the call to prayer at the mosque wakes her. She's been sweating in her sleep, but she doesn't mind. The heat makes sweat just more of the lushness. She's drawn to the sensuousness of the foliage here, the lustrous cries of birds. First thing today, she plans to pick up her pass from the brigadier, granting her permission to travel to the eastern province. She wants to research a subplot developing there between the guerrillas and the Muslims. You'd expect the guerrillas to strengthen their alliance with the Muslims with whom, for centuries, they've shared the same language and terrain, if not religion. But they've begun to harass the Muslims instead. In one particularly brutal incident, they sneaked into a Muslim town after dark, entered a mosque and murdered fifty worshippers at prayer.

When Elena goes out, the streets are bustling. She is part of the general surge upward through morning. Women tote bags of dal from the market, shopkeepers hustle their wares. The street is bright with saris and sarongs, schoolchildren in spotless, white uniforms. She likes the feel of burgeoning life insisting against the war's grain. Getting the pass is less a problem than traveling east. The train isn't safe, and by car the trip takes a day. But her contact in the brigadier's office owes her a favor. She manages to book a seat on one of the army's flights the next morning.

She packs, makes calls. On the way to dinner with the photographer she picks up a new notebook. After dinner she reads the mail on the balcony, then switches off the light. The pinprick stars come on one by one, filling the dark, a mist of faint dazzle. The captain's father was a biology teacher; their house was in the capital; both his sisters married to engineers. Still, the family must have lacked the connections to remove the captain to the safety of business or civil service. Or had he conceived of the service as duty? Or signed on for the money? The government pays its soldiers handsomely at a time when unemployment is high. He'd told her he'd wanted to go to law school, but had signed on with the army for a second tour. Once she'd asked him what music he liked. Coltrane, he'd said. Miles Davis.

His is a country wrung dry by colonial occupation, plagued for a decade by civil war between two dark skinned peoples, one Buddhist, one Hindu—and then there were Muslims who speak the Hindu's language. There has not been a war in her country for more than a century. She's enjoyed material comfort, education. She makes her living in a respected field, and the income gives her a fair amount of freedom. Should she choose not to marry, neither economic fact nor cultural custom will prevent this. If either she or the captain is in a position to exploit the other, surely it's she.

At the same time though, she's aware that part of her attractiveness may be due to scarcity. Purity in women is prized here, and the girls in that northern city wouldn't dream of getting involved with a soldier, no matter how handsome or persuasive. Women from the West, on the other hand, are thought to be available. Her acquiescence to what seems to her innocent play may in his eyes cast her in dubious light. Perhaps he perceives her as decadent, here where the word connotes not esprit but unbecoming behavior. Possibly he imagines he's exploiting her.

Or perhaps exploitation has nothing to do with it. She imagines the barracks, without amenity: a desk, papers, the phone. Beyond the window, that plain, earth wrung dry by fierce sun. The eye searches for a single tree, a clump of vegetation, any definition. The imagination paces, anxious, a length of longing. This is landscape that nudges the heart to dream. And at night the wash of moonlight like thin milk is tantalizing, its liquid sheen.

While she is free to come and go as she pleases, to choose or reject the photographer, the journalist, the Dutch attaché, the professor. Possibly her conversations with the captain are novelty, a form of amusement. She doesn't pretend this kind of exchange is beneath her, nor that she doesn't enjoy being the object of his lust. Anytime she feels like it she can slip her hand between her thighs and bring on their meeting in the swimming pool, the pleasure of water, the luster of his wet skin, the excitement lit in her by his importunate questions.

Of course she'd liked the color of his skin, its wet gleaming in the pool, like polished satinwood. But the Tamil journalist and the Sinhalese professor wear this same skin. And the Dutch attaché and the photographer have the healthy, glowing tans Westerners acquire with assiduous tennis. What attracts her to the captain is a matrix of circumstances, including the fact that their game offers both

MINE
142

safety and titillation, played as it is at a distance. The Canadian photographer, the Tamil journalist, the Dutch attaché and the Sinhalese professor have consequences. The captain presents only one consequence: the phone.

There is an edge of surreality to these conversations, as though the dream world, for a while, thrust into reality. Though their talk has beginning, middle, and end, this chronology takes place beyond the earth's turning, in psychic space where time is primordial. They inhabit their imaginations, terrain each manipulates at will. And in this landscape also there are no consequences. No assignations are consummated, no appointments missed. There is no hair in the drain, no gunfire in the distance, and no mines.

He hasn't told her how it happened. Was it in the jungle, walking, or in a vehicle, on a road? She thinks of that conference she'd covered in Lisbon on the technology of mine removal. There were engineers and military brass, as well as a number of private investors. The atmosphere had been decidedly upbeat. There had been much discussion of banning mines altogether, except for those designed to self-destruct. Though the countries with a monopoly on this technology were reluctant to transfer this knowledge to those without. Still, all participants seemed confident that the invention of gadgetry for quick and safe removal was only a matter of time. In the meantime, she'd thought, investors need not suffer. The production of mines and the service of their removal would continue to be lucrative.

She imagines the heat where he is, the barracks, those boots, the monotonous succession of days in uniform. Across this reverie the ringing of the phone is a blast.

"Elena. Were you asleep?"

"Of course," she lies. "Why aren't you asleep too?"

"I couldn't sleep. I thought of you lying in bed. I was thinking how loose your body must be when you're lying down. I was thinking how it would feel to touch your skin while you sleep. I wonder what you smell like right now. Tell me."

The plane arrives in the eastern capital before lunch. The heat is a monolith sliced by a length of lagoon. While the receptionist locates her reservation, she watches a breeze ripple the water. Its lapping sounds like mouths, whispering. She likes to think she'll fall asleep rocked by this sound, surrounded on one side by water, on the other by jungle. That green bulk in the distance makes her think of the prominent biologist who'd held a press conference to alert the public to the war's side effects. The reproductive cycles of sloths are interrupted by the thudding of mortars. The mongoose, wild boar, leopard and goanna get the jitters, which affects their reproduction as well. And the sleep patterns of pelicans, flamingos, and storks are disturbed, which in turn disturbs their nesting patterns. But it was elephants that had been uppermost in his mind. His was a culture in which the elephant was prized, and yet, as the war expanded, elephants were more and more likely to come upon mines.

The jungle areas, the receptionist tells her, are controlled by guerrillas. The army has secured the city and the surrounding villages, but at night guerrillas roam the countryside. No one, he warns, goes out after dark.

She lunches, then sets out. The heat is daunting. People move as though walking through blinding light. The trees are those with deep roots: palmyra, margosa. She walks beneath plumeria, passes here and there a hibiscus, its sudden gush of blossom startling, like a woman crying out.

The rippling sound of children's voices in the school yard suggests everything is going according to plan. But she notes a wariness in the eyes of adults, a weariness in the way they carry themselves. Then there are the stories told by those she interviews: the secretary of the city's peace committee, a Jesuit father, a physician. Nine fishermen, arrested by the army on suspicion of aiding the guerrillas, and never seen again. The local entrepreneur kidnapped by the guerrillas and held for ransom. Two high school girls who one day didn't make it home. School boys, lured by the excitement of propaganda videos, who run away and join the guerrillas. The army sergeant who threatened to rape a shopkeeper's daughter if her father didn't come up with a very large sum of money, then the girl's suicide, followed by the suicide of both parents.

And the farmer who died last week from a mine explosion in his own field.

At dusk she sits at a table near the water. Even as it rests in place the lagoon sways. Elena listens to the water's slap and sigh. From beyond the lagoon, the low boom of gunfire. Both sides set mines, the waiter tells her, and both commandeer civilians, when they can, to dig them up. A passing peasant wheeling his cart of firewood will do, or a laborer on his way to the dam project. Anyone who's handy can be organized for an hour, while three or four guards stroll the site's perimeter. Many farmers and fishermen, in the wrong place at the wrong time, have lost their lives. The waiter tells the one about the farmer commandeered by a lieutenant to dig up a mine—the same mine the guerrillas had forced him to plant in the first place.

When the waiter brings her check, he adds another anecdote. Edginess has increased since the guerrillas have taken to setting three mines together. Previously the lieutenant took his men off to the side where they watched the unfortunate peasant they'd forced perform his delicate labor. Now the guerrillas wire three mines together, one in the road and the others on either side. If the one in the road blows, they all blow, taking the lieutenant and his men with them. Just last week, the waiter says, there was such an incident.

She goes to her room, reads, then turns out the light. Dark has the texture of satin, a black dress pooled on the floor. Slowly the gibbous moon rises. She's aware of her body, creamy in this light, her breath that live place where over and over what's inside her touches the world. All this abundance put into the universe, and for what? For destruction, she thinks, in the continuously wheeling cycle.

When the phone rings, Elena speaks first. "Is there gunfire where you are?"

"Not tonight."

"There's gunfire here."

"Don't worry. The guerrillas there won't come into town. Here they've been lying low for weeks. There's not much to do. Paperwork." Suddenly longing threads his voice. "I wish I could see you." She hears the ache, feels it tugging her.

"I'm going back the day after tomorrow," she says.

"I'll call you there, that night," he says. "But now, right now, what are you doing? Are you lying down?"

"Yes," she says. "I was trying to go to sleep."

"Tell me the truth," he says. "Have you met someone there? Tell me where you go to meet him. Does he have a vehicle? Tell me what he looks like. Tell me what he likes. I want to know the details. You know I need to talk to you. Tell me."

She wakes sweating, sticky. Outside her window, running water. She pulls back the curtain. An attendant with a hose waters the bougainvillaea. Magenta, she thinks, is a sexual color, a color without diffidence, without hesitation.

The lagoon is a mirror thrown down across sand. She takes a taxi to the nearby Muslim town where the massacre occurred. Members of the mosque committee point out the bullet holes in the walls, the uneven places in the floor where blood pooled. The pillar behind which the Imam stood to escape death. They point out the list of names posted at the entrance. One of the dead was an exceptional twelve-year-old boy who could recite long passages of the Koran by heart.

She imagines the sound of cloth, ripped away. She has been present when bereft women have torn their clothing. And the women here, did they keen?

That same afternoon, while she inspects the mosque, guerrillas farther south stop a bus, take off the Muslims— men, women, children—line them up by the side of the road. Then the execution. She sits at a table, sipping arrack, when the waiter brings this news. The sun is setting over the lagoon, wisps of pastel shading toward dark. She thinks of the list of names, the plaque.

When the captain calls, Elena tells him this news.

"Why are the guerrillas turning on the Muslims? They have no quarrel. They speak the same language."

"It's a kind of suicide. The guerrillas know they can't last."

"You can feel the fear here," she says. "What about you, Mendis?" Without planning to, she has spoken his name. "Are you ever afraid?"

"Sometimes, yes." He pauses. She imagines his body at that instant, its breathy energy, the beat of blood at his throat. "The rest of the time I don't think about it."

"How did your knee get hurt?" she asks. She is pushing with these questions. She wants their words to spiral wider, to somehow, impossibly, deliver him to her. "You said a mine."

"We were in a vehicle. Myself and three others. I was in back, farthest away. The left front tire hit it. The driver was killed."

"Lucky it wasn't you."

"No. It was my friend."

"Your friend. Oh, I'm sorry."

"I was supposed to drive. But I felt sleepy. So he told me to get in back."

Her exclamation is a single syllable.

"Don't worry about it," he says.

"I'm sorry for your friend, but I'm glad you were in back. You were lucky."

"I'm lucky now, Elena. I'm talking to you. Promise you won't stop talking to me."

She laughs. "I promise."

"Tell me about your new lover. Is he a guerrilla? Or a civilian? A boy in the army?"

"None of the above!" She laughs at this notion that she flits from assignation to assignation. But this line of questioning is part of his tactic, meant to encourage erotic discourse, to inflame imagination.

"How many times did you do it with him? Did you go with him in his vehicle? Did he take you to his friends? Did you do it with them too? How many men were there, Elena? Tell me."

She's been warned that the train can be dangerous. The guerrillas need to finance their operations. Sometimes they stop a train and rob passengers. But she can't get a flight out for three more days. And she prefers to be among other travelers, her sweat just more of the collective humidity, herself of the mesh. The car is crowded, but she has a window seat, and water. They roll past paddy fields, groves of coconut palms. The train stops twice at checkpoints. Soldiers board, search baggage for weapons, confiscate batteries which the guerrillas use to build mines.

The landscape of drought rolls by, sand and distance, the occasional village. Eventually the rocking lulls her to sleep. When the train stops, she wakes. The woman beside her touches her arm, then points. Outside, a line of guerrillas stands guard. From two cars ahead, the sound of voices. Scuffling. Now four guerrillas make nine Muslim men and women get down, herd them away from the tracks.

She feels a rill of fear sweep the car. People call out in muted voices. A baby begins to cry. Suddenly a Hindu turns to the Muslim beside him and gestures, suggesting the man take off his toppi. The Hindu takes it, slips it in his bag. Quickly others hide the men's toppis, the women's purdah. Some of the Hindu women stick puttus on the Muslim women's foreheads. They take the Muslim babies on their laps.

Through the car, the electricity of hopeful conspiracy. Now the door is flung open. Two guerrillas enter, mouths masked with black cloth, rifles ready. Quickly they survey the car. Their glances, boiling water flung through the air. Where are the Muslims? One of the guerrillas accosts a passenger, his questions quick thrusts. The man shakes his head, his voice deferential. The guerrilla grabs him by the shirt, yanks him up.

Then, in the distance, the first shots. The guerrillas tense toward the sound. The one doing the interrogation curses. Both jump down, run with the others into the trees.

O happy gift of being unharmed, sweet grant of ordinary existence! Fear in the car flows out like water down a gully. People call out to each other. Some embrace. Some take food from their bags. One man distributes candy to the children. Another, with a bottle of arrack, goes down the aisle, offering it. The woman beside Elena offers her rice wrapped in a banana leaf. Elena gives her biscuits in return. A little boy across the aisle watches her, shyly. She gives him a Coke from her pack.

When the soldiers arrive, they joke with the conductor, take the names of those who were pulled from the train. Then they send the train on.

There is gaiety in the air: they have escaped. Elena loosens with the others, salutes the pleasurable savor of sweat, and this simple, amazing mechanism, the breath. How could she have taken the body for granted! She is here, in the flesh, its weariness, its elation, its ebb and flow through the wash of moments. Her relief is elixir, and she drinks the glass to the bottom.

And as they roll west, as the desert turns into jungle, it comes to her that she must meet the captain. Their game played at a distance will no longer be amusing. The longing in his voice is still with her, ink coloring its way through the blood. And yes, she too longs. She must have a face and hands, a voice speaking beside her. They're alive, after all, in delicious bodies. Who could have devised so cunningly such pleasure! She decides she will arrange to go north. They will slide back and forth in the turquoise water, two slick fish gliding toward evening. And in the darker water of evening, liquid and exultant, they will try each other's bodies.

She does not forget that events sometimes disappoint us. Still there is no reason they should not investigate their moment, make that little escape from the world's mesh, from roles laid out for them like clothes by others. She's aware of her blossomy body, its temperature, its softness. Slowly the moon rises over the jungle, and she imagines the captain unable to sleep. He's taken off his shirt. The boots are hot, but he keeps them on in case he has to move fast. If he could call her now, she would tell him she's coming. She imagines his excitement. And wonders: what would he say?

Before leaving the station she buys a ticket to that northern city for the day after tomorrow. Outside in the glare, hawkers offer bangles, T-shirts. The light intensifies toward noon, liquid rising to the lip of its pitcher. Heat interrogates the street. Elena hails a taxi, climbs in. They pass stalls where women string plumeria garlands, a temple where three monks in orange robes descend.

The nurse has left her a note and some leftover curry. Jasmine beside the window smells as though its been heated. She showers, then naps. Through afternoon she works on the story, then dines with the photographer, works again until ten. The moon has risen over the wall. Leaves murmur and lap the dark. That jasmine vine is there, beyond the window. She lies back in scented drowsiness.

In her dream she walks beside the ocean. Breakers crash down across sand. Now her golden retriever from childhood, dead these many years, emerges from surf. In fiery sun he bounds toward her, salt glazed, dragging something wet and black in his teeth.

She wakes to the cry of a parrot. Slowly at first, then more quickly, she understands: there was no call. She showers and dresses, takes a bus to the paper where the Tamil journalist writes a column. The story has come over the wire. Ten men, one mine. Six wounded, one dead. From the neutrality of print the captain's name rises like the blare of a siren.

Breath is an animal that follows you everywhere. The journalist occupies himself with certain papers. She walks to the window. Around her, the nearly inaudible tick heat makes as it climbs toward the zenith. Beyond the traffic a flame tree blossoms. She thinks of those village women trained by U.N. aides to remove mines themselves from their fields. It's one of those things she'll probably never have to do.

And this mine: was it produced in her country? But it might have come from Britain, South Africa, India. China. It might have been one of the handmade models manufactured by the guerrillas. She tries out the idea that at this moment he might be safe in his barracks, she caught in crossfire not meant for her. But that would have been not the rule but the exception. She a journalist from the richest country on the planet, he a soldier in a small nation racked by civil war.

Given these circumstances, what would love have been? What it always is, she thinks. The unexpected swoop of feeling, the gift you didn't plan. Those Hindu women reaching out to take the Muslim babies. But Mendis hadn't been with her on the train. She couldn't turn to him, touch his hand, whisper. Instead she'd offered the woman beside her biscuits. She'd given a little boy a Coke.

EATING GOD

3

DISTANT LIGHTS ON WATER

Passing the Museum, Clayton saw the panhandler, a woman, leaning against the polished fascia. She wore a thin wool dress, shiny with wear. Beside her a plastic mug, much battered. Daffodils bloomed in planters flanking the steps, and Clayton experienced a pleasant sense of accumulating wealth amidst these intimations of spring. And there was the woman, in watery light. It was as though someone had placed her against the facade, as though she and the light had been composed.

Clayton had met his wife, Celia, a photographer, at a gallery opening. She was enjoying the ease and the challenge that went with early success, and Clayton had begun to rise through the ranks in a design line that enjoyed a commanding presence in women's fashion. Celia's series, *Light on Water*, was a study in chiaroscuro. Nuance made a difference. He noted how small increments of increase or decrease in aperture changed things the light fell upon, how these increments moved the viewer back and forth between shallows, depths. Nuance informed Celia's breadth, wide as the arched span of horizon from pole to pole. She made him think of earth's curvature, how ships going away from land become tiny until they disappear.

His company dealt in a volume that required manufacturing outlets in several Third World countries where Clayton sometimes gave coins to beggars on the street. Some had lost limbs. All were thin in a way that suggested they had seldom had enough to eat. Some had children who were importunate but listless, as though already they lived without hope. Now he reached into his pocket, dropped his change into the woman's cup. Light reflected by stone seemed to swirl toward him, enclosing him in its warmth. It was a nice moment, and he savored it.

As a child he'd been fascinated by flecks of light floating like a mist near the ceiling: his grandmother's chandelier. The many bits shimmered, far away, like lights seen across water, and he gazed up, aching. Eventually he'd understood this light came from a lamp suspended from the ceiling, a thing one didn't take down and hold. His longing was nearly bearable then, and he felt pride because he understood you didn't ask grown-ups for the impossible. Still he longed to bring it closer, to be, if he could, inside it, suffused with that watery light. He indulged this longing while his parents and grandmother sat in the next room, their conversation a murmur drifting over the dessert plates toward him. He'd been aware in those moments of their great distance from him. They'd had no idea what wealth he almost possessed.

What he didn't know, because his mother had never told anyone, was that once he'd nearly drowned. He'd been two, toddling beside her, and had fallen into a ditch. The water in the ditch was a turbulent force. He'd gone under and begun to float down with the current. What his mother didn't know was that to him the water had seemed another moving body, holding him. It was then, at the end of what seemed a dark tunnel, that he'd seen light, an appealing disc of flickering brightness—light dissolved into hundreds of dreamy flecks. He was an arc, reaching out, yearning toward the lit distance. But his mother, infused by terror with strength, had snatched him back, lifted him by the feet. Water had poured from his mouth. He had begun to cry, to breathe.

On Sunday afternoon Celia returned from Yunnan where she'd photographed Yi warriors for a *National Geographic* article. The sound of her humming while she unpacked reminded him of the chandelier, its thousand vibrating bits. He was in awe of her poise. Her profile and the slope of her shoulder in shadow were foreground. Behind her lay the river, light at low slant.

"Massage my shoulders, will you, sweet? I'm a wreck." She spoke from the nebula of her warmth. Celia had been drawn to him by his excitement over her photographs. He did not find enthusiasm embarrassing. And he was without the impulse—too often the case with her editors—to maintain a certain aloof distance. He went about life energetically, with a natural verve which matched her own.

When he'd loosened her shoulders, she rolled onto her back. Celia wore jeans when she worked, or, in the tropics, cotton safari gear, but she liked to tease Clayton, saying she'd married him for his clothes.

"I brought you a dress," he said. It was a joke between them. He often brought her some new item from his line, and each time they pretended it was the first time he'd done this.

"A dress! Aren't you amazing," she said, laughing. She lay between him and the window. Beyond, the river gleamed.

"Here, let me undress you. You can try it on." She laughed again, and he reached to unbutton her blouse. They were at play, and gradually, as they made love, he felt himself arriving at the center of a sphere, around which the rest of space floated.

When Clayton saw the man at the subway entrance holding out his cap, he was aware that he was glad to see him. It was the end of a productive day, and the little pleasure of going without a jacket suggested a lightness in all things. A little boy stood beside the man, clutching his pants leg.

"Spare some change?" the man asked. Clayton was conscious, suddenly, of what he was doing, in the same way that, when he began to make love to his wife, he was conscious of rising out of some thick medium in which he'd been submerged, into another, lighter medium. He reached into his pocket. He had nothing smaller than twenties. On impulse he thrust the whole role of bills into the man's cap.

"Brother!" the man said. "God bless!" It was as though the air and light had parted for Clayton's thrust hand, then enveloped him. "You some brother!" the man said. Clayton reached out and squeezed the man's shoulder.

"My pleasure," he said. Then he walked on. Who would have thought something so simple, something people thought of as a charitable and a human, if minor, duty, could deliver so much naked pleasure? How had he got so far away from this kind of spontaneous joy? His work, of course, was predictable. It was a matter of mediating design and markets, and there was nothing spontaneous about this calculation. He felt himself in the throes of a decision. But what decision? To bankroll every homeless wanderer who crossed his path? That would be folly, he thought, then changed his mind. Possibly it wasn't folly, but neither was it exactly the point.

When he'd traveled in his student days, places of worship had drawn him. He would enter and sit in awe of the simplicity of huge Buddhas. The temples of Hindu goddesses intrigued him, the quiet of mosques, the sacral splendor of cathedrals. In these spaces, grandly conceived and splendidly executed, he'd felt himself again beneath that chandelier's dispersing brightness. Now he thought there was something ineffable but crucial about the act of letting money go. It provided an immediate lightening of the atmosphere. He walked on, rising into the deep and detailed texture of the day.

On his first trip abroad, after he'd negotiated the business at hand with de Souza, the manager, and his assistants, Clayton decided to visit the factory's sewing room. De Souza, a jovial man in his fifties, accompanied Clayton. The room resembled a warehouse. It was without amenity, except for the women. Their clothing wrapped them decorously. Sitting at state-of-the-art Japanese sewing machines, stitching the tailored, often daring, garments women in Europe and America would wear, they resembled commercial versions of nuns. De Souza pointed out that the women were only allowed to work because their families couldn't survive without the additional income.

"It's a pity," de Souza said. "Some are children themselves, fifteen years old, or sixteen."

Clayton thought the lighting above the machines a bit dim. Couldn't they upgrade the system? De Souza demurred.

"These things cost money."

"Do it," Clayton said. When de Souza looked at him doubtfully, he spoke. "I'll take responsibility."

A secretary appeared to summon de Souza back to his office, but Clayton lingered, watching a seamstress guide cloth through the feed. Clayton leaned down.

"How many hours a day do you work?"

She didn't understand. The woman next to her leaned forward.

"Twelve hours," she said. A fierceness in her eyes made Clayton think of Celia's photographs, of her subject's suspicion, anxiousness. Anger. "Sometimes they make rush and we have to work faster. We have to say please like children to go to bathroom." She spoke hurriedly, glancing toward the door as though she expected de Souza to return and chastise her. "And we get sick from cotton."

She extended her hand, gesturing toward the air. In the spray of light from one high window Clayton saw for the first time the motes floating. Now he noticed that some of the seamstresses wore cloth masks. He felt the embarrassing weight of his naivete. This slackness about the venue, he decided, was negligence on the part of the local managers. He found de Souza and explained what needed to be done.

"It would be expensive," De Souza said. He seemed anxious. "Some elaborate system of fans and filters. Your company won't pay for this."

On the flight back Clayton watched the plane's wing, cutting through silvered light. This glancing brilliance— the very fact of flight, now so commonplace—served to remind him of his context. He came from a country that could afford to extend aid to other countries. Some small changes—fewer hours, an increase in wages, upgrading the sewing rooms—wouldn't cost so much that his fellows could refuse.

The first few days back he used his bankroll of camaraderie to lay the groundwork for the proposals he intended to submit at the first meeting. When that day came, the others went along with the lighting improvements, since Clayton presented this as a fait accompli. But they treated his other suggestions as outré.

"Give us a break," one said, laughing. "We're not a nonprofit. Besides, their government gets aid in the millions. What happened? You run into Mother Teresa?"

"I've been there," another said, "and those people are happy. Those factories aren't palaces, but we've got letters in the files thanking us for giving them work. We're giving poor people jobs, Clayton."

"They have to live in the Free Trade Zones," Clayton said. "Six to a tiny room. They're lucky to get two days off in two months to see their kids. And families mean everything to these people."

"So now they get to buy their kids things," said the one who had been Clayton's closest ally. "It's a trade-off."

They liked Clayton and wanted to humor him. The company gave small bonuses occasionally, and one of the partners suggested that on his next trip abroad he should distribute a bonus to the workers. As they filed out, several of them clapped him on the back. He was one of them, and they welcomed him back. But the feeling swept over him that he'd been chastened. He walked back to his office, taking in the fact: all he'd got for the women was the promise of a small, onetime bonus. The irony, he thought, was that if he'd asked for a raise for himself, they'd probably have agreed.

"You were brave and wonderful to challenge those greedy bastards," Celia said.

They were drinking maté she'd brought from Brazil and watching the sun set beyond the river. For weeks Clayton had been disconsolate. He'd continued to press his partners to use a percentage of profits to better conditions for their employees abroad. But his persistence had no effect. He berated himself. There seemed no way not to be who he was, someone born to privilege, making his living at the expense of others—women!—forced by circumstance to accept pittance wages.

At Clayton's request, the accountant had given him access to computer files, and Clayton poured over them, hesitantly at first, then more methodically. He was looking for anything that might give him leverage. Though his expertise was not in finance, he was conversant with the company's assets and liabilities. He'd focused on the fact that rather than subcontracting the work, his line owned the foreign factories. The local managers were the company's employees. And the figures showed that the line was doing very well indeed. They could well afford to transfer ownership to the locals, he thought. His company would buy from them, and the locals could realize a profit. His line would still profit as well. There looked to be ample funds for this kind of gesture, and he toyed with the idea of proposing it. But he guessed what the likely response would be. His partners would resist, out of habit.

He'd begun walking to work. It gave him space to brood. While he walked he thought of Celia photographing vanishing species, clouds of oil fires, ships dumping refuse into the gardens of whales. Amidst the fanning leaves of banana trees, the hierophany of sand and water, the sloping hills of polar snow, she was in her element. The concentrated intensity she brought to her work was a form of love. He wanted to approach his work with that same attentiveness.

"It isn't just my partners," he said. "It's how business is. It's part of the territory."

Celia, he thought, had encountered more facets of life than he had, and she had done it at eye level. She'd dined with duchesses, slept among the families of nomadic herdsmen, returned the gaze of reptiles, deer. Though it wasn't just that her experience was wider than his. It had something to do with her intelligence about that experience. What she learned seemed to make her both more multitudinous and at the same time more pragmatic.

"My situation's not so different from yours," Celia said. "I photograph a grizzly, but just to get there I've broken trail. Or I cover the Kurds in exile, but to do it I have to impinge on them. There I am with my expensive equipment, coolly recording their private moments. They accept this and offer me tea. Sure, I bring the plight of grizzlies and Kurds to the attention of the audience of whatever magazine I'm shooting for, but without them I haven't got a subject."

When he walked now, he carried cash to give away. Often those to whom he gave money offered gifts in return. A stick of gum, cigarettes, flowers plucked from public gardens. Today he'd come home carrying a plastic horse with one ear broken off. He told Celia how the boy had thrust it toward him. Clayton had observed that the boy was in the embrace of the lifting pleasure that came with giving. It felt like unbinding the sails of a skiff, running them up the mast. He took the gift and thanked the boy, then offered it back. But the child grinned and hid behind his mother. Clayton tried to return the toy to the mother, but she insisted her son wanted him to have it. The boy had peeped

STORIES BY MARILYN KRYSL

from behind his mother's skirt, eyes alight with bravura and joy.

Celia had always given spare change to panhandlers. Obviously they needed it. She did not think much about it and soon forgot what she'd given and to whom. Now she kissed Clayton's cheek. "You don't lock your doors," she said. She'd never told him that at the time she'd agreed to marry him, she'd had a premonition: he would do something surprising, something spectacular. She had not tried to guess what it might be, but it was as though she'd made an oracular note to herself. He would do some grand and glittering deed. She was sure of it.

"Remember the moose calf? It was when I'd gone to Finland. The mother was grazing, and the little one had wandered off to the side. I put out my hand, on impulse, and the calf stuck out her big tongue and licked me."

He kept up his campaign at the office. The others teased him. "You're going to turn into a bleeding heart hippie," one said.

"Try sleeping on the street, Clayton," another partner joked. "One night. No foam mattress. No sleep mask. No Courvoisier. I dare you."

Once he might have enjoyed their challenges. Now he entertained the notion that he no longer fit. Partly dissatisfied, partly curious, he went so far as to inquire about a job at one of the local shelters for the homeless. He phoned, assuming there'd be those with M.A.s in social work ahead of him. When he got routed to the Department of Social Services, the head informed him that most salaried slots, sparse to begin with, had been cut. The salaries, where they still existed, were so minimal as to be token.

And there were batteries of applications on file in the event a position came open.

"Most slots are manned by volunteers," the woman told him. "If you care to volunteer, just phone the shelter of your choice."

Walking home that afternoon, Clayton gave a handful of ones to a woman with a baby. Temperatures were in the nineties and would probably stay that way through the night. Geraniums bloomed in pots beside walkups. He thought of stopping off for a beer. Then a man seated on a black plastic garbage bag on the sidewalk caught his eye. On a whim Clayton sat down beside him.

"Hotter than hell itself," Clayton said. It was an opener. They chatted, and the man produced two cigarettes from his shirt pocket and offered one to Clayton. He slid over to offer space on the garbage bag.

"No sense ruining that suit," he said.

Clayton smiled, and moved over. They smoked in silence. From this angle the city looked to be all legs. They were strong, healthy legs, and they had destinations, obligations. Holdings. Clayton was aware that his silk shirt was an impeccable antique white. Suddenly the man turned to Clayton and patted him on the shoulder. He leaned closer, in conspiratorial pose. "Friend," he said, "you don't belong here."

Clayton sold his golf clubs.

"Why?" Celia asked.

"The game doesn't interest me much. They were sitting around, collecting dust."

She watched him sort his wardrobe, separating what he felt he no longer needed into plastic bags. Occasionally she photographed him the way you might a loved one. But often, when the impulse struck her, she didn't follow through but demurred, knowing her impulse came from affection, sensing it was not the moment for a definitive portrait.

"Let's divest!" Celia said, teasing him. She studied the clothes in her closet, then began to lift out dresses he'd given her which now were out of fashion. "But how can I give these away? They were love gifts."

Clayton laughed. "I'll bring you more," he said.

"That's just it. You can," she said.

Still she got into the spirit. She kept two dresses, some sweaters, her safari clothes, jeans. He loaded the Audi with clothes, some books and tapes, drove to one of the shelters and gave the young man in charge his cargo. At home again, he turned his attention to the Audi. Did they need it? Mostly they drove it to the terminal parking lot, to have it waiting at the end of return flights.

"Sweetheart," she said, "we can afford it. It's a convenience."

"But the rest of the time it just sits there."

"Is that really the reason you want to get rid of it?"

Clayton frowned. "It's just as convenient to take a taxi. We can afford that too."

"There isn't any way not to do damage," Celia said.

"Of course not. But we can minimize our damage," he said. "I think you want that too."

She was grateful for his honesty. "Oh why not. Sell it, if it pleases you. I can get into this."

"Let's not give each other Christmas presents this year," Clayton said. He looked through papers for the Audi's title.

"Fine with me," Celia said. "There's nothing I want. We could walk around Christmas day and give away some little presents." She ran water in the kettle and set it on the stove. Now his attractiveness included a distracted quality. He was not tranquil. She wanted to photograph him now, she who had recorded the faces of Mongolian shepherds, refugees, the honchos of guerrilla movements.

His destination was a country in which two groups of dark-skinned people who spoke different languages were at war. For more than a century civil servants of the ruling European power had administered the government. Now the royal family of that ruling power was no longer welcome in this country. In the neighboring country the American president's limousine had been stoned, and in a third a Fulbright scholar had been murdered.

Warfare in this country was generally confined to outlying areas, but, just days before, a high-ranking naval officer had been murdered in the capital by a suicide bomber on a motorcycle. The bomber had passed just as the officer and two subordinates were getting into their vehicle. Along with a handful of bystanders they had all been killed.

Clayton had picked a small hotel in a part of town away from tourists. He registered, then strolled out into evening. Here in the capital you wouldn't suspect there was war raging in the north. He walked amidst women toting string bags of eggplant and plantain. Lively hawkers cried up their bangles and combs, toothpaste and small gilded idols. Walking, he was conscious of the press of bodies. In the street taxis, buses, auto-rickshaws, trucks, and bicycles jockeyed for space.

People were intent on their business in a way that bespoke urgency. He walked through streets strewn with bits of trash to a nearby market. Amidst the colors of eggplants and peppers in stalls, he became aware of a voice, rising in pitch. Behind a stall stacked with onions and tomatoes a woman shouted at her small daughter. The woman held a stout length of wood and had raised it above her head as though to strike. The girl cowered, her face bewildered. Clayton heard in the woman's voice the shrillness of someone pushed to their limits. The little girl began to weep.

Suddenly the mother threw down the wood, turned her back, and began to stack onions. Clayton turned away. Outside the market he walked, wanting to erase the scene, knowing he couldn't but walking anyway, as though to separate himself from anguish.

That night it rained. The next day was bright with the white light that characterizes tropical latitudes. Clayton took a taxi through streets littered with garbage. At the factory he met with the manager, Mr. Mallalingam, and his assistants. There were more of them than Clayton could keep straight, but that was the custom. There were always more on the payroll than the job required. Some were probably relatives, others men to whom Mallalingam owed a favor.

Tea and sweets were brought in, and Clayton made the necessary small talk about family. And how was business, he asked then. Mallalingam shook his head, frowning. The company had received a letter from a group of seamstresses. He lifted a piece of paper from his file. Imagine, they believed they were forming a union!

"What are their complaints?" Clayton asked.

Mallalingam hesitated. Then he read from the letter. "Piecework wages are less than legal minimum. No over-time pay."

"Is that true?"

Mallalingam looked pained. "They are paid sufficiently for their needs," he said. "These things were agreed upon by your company. It's enough." His expression turned disconsolate, then offended. "These women also say insults from management. And another complaint—but this is preposterous—threats." His air was that of a man whose pride has been deeply wounded.

"Being laid off?" Clayton said.

"No one has ever threatened these women," Mallalingam said. "They are being incited to this by agitators." He spoke as though a great weight had been placed on his shoulders. "Now we must deal with these outside elements."

"You know for a fact that their discontent is manufactured by others?"

"The government has had to contend with these elements for some time. But how unfortunate for the women. Some of them will suffer in the process of sorting this out."

"Let's meet with the women while I'm here," Clayton said. "I'd like to get their side of the story first hand."

Mallalingam's body went blank, as though a sliding door had been closed. "Please don't trouble yourself over this. Please, no." He held up his hand. "You should not be burdened. We will settle the matter in a satisfactory manner. Enjoy your visit. Tomorrow you can travel to the shore, if you like. We will send a car for you."

Propriety demanded that Clayton cede to Mallalingam, but he declined the car. Then he took Mallalingam and two of his assistants to lunch. At the restaurant he explained he wanted to distribute a small bonus to the seamstresses. Actually it was a rather larger bonus than his company had provided. He'd added to it a year's interest on his own stocks. It made the bonuses worth the trouble.

"This is very kind of your company, very kind!" Mallalingam was effusive. "It may solve our problem. Your generosity will perhaps persuade the women to back down."

Clayton hesitated. He did not want to be party to manipulation. But he had come especially with this bonus in mind, and he'd changed the funds into local currency. Back at the factory he asked the secretary accompanying him to explain to the women that this bonus should in no way influence their negotiations with management. "This bonus is a gift," he said. "No strings attached." The two of them entered from the back of the sewing room. Lined up, the women resembled manufactured goods stored temporarily for shipping. They wore printed cotton saris, and their black hair was plaited down their backs or wound like a crown. The secretary turned off the music. She spoke over the P.A. system in the native language. Then she turned the music back on, and the women began to sew again.

He walked down the rows, handing out envelopes. The women's hands were small, like the hands of children. A few smiled at him. Most took the envelope shyly, then dropped their gaze. He'd expected their circumspection. He hadn't expected the light coming off their faces. When he came close, the atmosphere softened and turned lustrous, like light swirling down through the surface of water.

His sense of his surroundings was heightened by the details he now observed: the lint in the air, the loud music which kept the women from chatting, the number of women coughing, the strain he observed in their bodies.

They could not escape their need for employment, and he could not separate himself from his own and his people's history. Though he gave these women little bits of coinage in a gesture of protest, he remained one of those who took away with one hand what he gave with the other. He was, as the phrase went, part of the problem.

And yet, as he passed out the envelopes, the familiar rill of energy rose in him, and the light around him and each woman he reached toward cast itself beyond them, illuminating the dimness. Though the exchange involved money, there were those moments in which it obliterated money. Two people who had seemed isolated beings rose and entered a single gestalt.

He handed the last envelope to the last seamstress. Now he was at the front of the room. Suddenly the P.A. system went silent. A woman near the back stood and began to sing. The others rose as a body, singing. Some of them looked at him as they sang, but others stared straight ahead. Though the melody was familiar, he could not understand the words. But he was moved. This was their gift to him.

Outside it was twilight. He got out of the taxi while it was still some distance from his hotel. At a market he stopped beside a vendor selling mangos. The globes of fruit, one on another, seemed alive, and the air, when he reached to take one, was a permeable medium that opened to receive his reaching arm. The vendor was eager with a child's hopefulness. He helped Clayton choose the best fruits, slipped them into a plastic bag.

Clayton noticed coming toward him a little girl holding her mother's hand. She was probably seven or eight. She smiled at him, and her eyes flashed, as though with some splendid secret. Children often rushed toward him, beggar's children taught to importune, wanting coins, bills, a pen. But when she was beside him, the girl reached out. For a moment her small hand grasped his wrist. It was a gesture of affectionate, fleeting possession. She held on a moment, smiled, then let go.

He watched the girl and her mother out of sight. She'd wanted nothing from him. Even in children such purity of impulse was soon lost. He'd been offered something, spontaneously and freely, here where there was little left over with which to be kind. But generosity was a different currency, he thought, replete and multiplying. You were not diminished by it. He walked past workers waiting for buses, not caring where he walked as long as the sensation of her hand on his skin lasted. Beyond the city's lights he could see faint stars. There was a shimmering in this dark, which, if you looked closely, seemed lit bits of tingling brightness. He looked, but he couldn't find a line of demarcation between the dark and this shimmering. There was light and there was darkness and both were part of the seamlessness of the world.

He hailed a taxi, climbed in, and gave the driver the address of his hotel. It was only in the taxi, when he heard on the radio the melody the women had sung, that he registered what one of the managers, earlier in the day, had told him. They'd instituted the singing of a song as closure to the workday for each shift. The suggestion, he'd said, had come down in a memo from Clayton's home office. The song was the people's national anthem. The women sang it every day.

Giving out the envelopes had seemed innocent and hopeful, a repeated gesture like a mantram or the thousands of prostrations Buddhists performed. But this repetition of the anthem had a troubling slant. One of his partners had calculated that associating the anthem with the factory would rally the women to accept their circumstances. It was a way of associating the foreign company with the workers' own nation, so that the prominence of Western executives might be obscured, though, like puppeteers, they pulled the strings.

He woke and decided he would check in once more at the factory. He would have liked to indulge in a swim, and his flight did not leave until late afternoon, but he wanted to chat once more with Mallalingam. Perhaps he could get a clearer picture of the women's situation, find out how Mallalingam intended to address their demands.

He took a taxi to the Free Trade Zone. Traffic seemed more congested than usual, and as they approached the factory it became impossible to proceed. Cars and buses stalled. By leaning out the window Clayton was able to see police at the factory entrance, not just one or two, but a squad with batons.

He paid the driver and hurried to where the officers blocked the entrance. A sergeant who spoke English informed Clayton that there was "rioting" inside. Clayton produced his card and convinced the man that he was indeed an executive of the company. The officer sent for someone to accompany him. Instead of Mallalingam himself, one of his underlings came. What was his name? Clayton was afraid to guess and get it wrong.

"Come," the man said. "We will go to Mr. Mallalingam's office." Clayton followed him down a familiar hallway.

"I hope no one's been hurt," Clayton said.

"The ladies would not cooperate. We could not convince them to return to work. Now they are talking with Mallalingam. We will wait for his report in the office."

"Can you take me where he is?" Clayton said. "I'd like to get a feel for the situation."

"He does not want you to take risks. You are valuable," the man said, attempting a joke.

They were about to pass another hallway, down which Clayton could hear voices. When they were opposite the hallway, he glanced left, saw police bunched outside a doorway. There were always more police than were needed. On impulse Clayton went striding down this hall. When the police saw him, they seemed uncertain what to do. Clayton tried to see over their heads, but he could see only police. Then he heard the sound of shattering china, and Mallalingam burst through, pushing past the press of men in uniform.

Through the breach Clayton glimpsed the women still inside, diminutive figures around a table, and in front of each a cup of tea. There was something innocent about this scene, but Mallalingam's face was flushed, though whether with confusion, anger, or both, Clayton could not tell. Mallalingam saw him. He reached out and tugged at Clayton's arm, shouting something Clayton didn't understand. A police whistle blared, and a new phalanx of uniformed officers pushed past them, into the room. These men wore helmets and black kerchiefs across their mouths, and they carried white plastic buckets with lids. Clayton was just able to glimpse two of the women: their faces registered fear. Quickly they stood and tried to get to the door.

A stench filled the air. Could it be? But of course, yes. The buckets had been opened, and now the men reached gloved hands into the excrement and began to throw it at the women, to smear it on the saris of those closest to them. The women's cries were pitched high, and in the melee he saw two of the masked men push a woman's head down.

A third smeared her face and ears. Clayton lunged. He shouted. He would go to the center, climb on the table and there get the attention of the officers. Then Mallalingam was beside him.

"Please. We must not interfere with police."

"Police!" Clayton said. "These men aren't police!" He pushed into the press of bodies. One whole bucket spilled across the table, its contents smearing the folds of a woman's pink sari. The masked officers seemed for the first time to register his presence.

"Go!" he shouted. He banged his fist on the table. "Get out!"

The one with the whistle blew another sharp blast, and in moments the phalanx was out of the room, running in squad formation down the hallway. Clayton stood there, excrement on his hands, his clothes. He was surrounded by women, sobbing, bent over, unwilling to look at him, trying to hide their shame.

The plane taxied in. Clayton thought of the little girls: the one cowering, the one who had touched his wrist. He remembered how in the light from those shops, the dark gold of peoples' skin had seemed to throb, how the whites of their eyes flickered and swayed like distant lights on water. The seat belt sign blinked off, and the passengers in front of him began to file out. He walked toward the gate, leaning forward, looking for Celia. She saw him and waved. They made their way to each other and embraced.

"You're lit up," she said. "Good things happened?"

"I don't know whether something good happened," he said. "There were some absolutely astounding events— starting with the seamstresses wanting a union."

He gave her the short version. "I felt like I was being given an education. I'll have to probe. I don't know yet how bad we are, or who's responsible. Is Mallalingam following our orders, or is he the prime mover? And is this an anomaly or what routinely happens?"

Celia nodded. "On my trip to Dar es Salaam, a civil servant told me his government used to purchase weapons from the Israelis, while the separatists bought from the Russians through a London-Turkey supplier. Now a German munitions firm—the major shareholder's an American—contracts with both sides."

"Business as usual," he said. "How have you been?"

"Well," she replied. "And at your elbow. I'm with you, wherever you go."

He laughed. "And where shall we go, elbow to elbow?"

"How about home to the apartment?"

He nodded. "By the way, I've been wondering. Should we keep the apartment?"

"Absolutely," Celia said. "Though we cast aside our silks and our emeralds, I still need the apartment to come home to."

She stopped and turned to him. "It's better that you're present at board meetings, plugging your view," she said. "The gadfly effect."

"Is that the best I can do?"

Celia remembered her premonition: Clayton would accomplish something magnificent. Now this notion struck her as sentimental. What had she expected? A blaze of trumpets? A Hollywood spectacular?

"I like to think I haven't seen your best yet," she said. "Or mine. But maybe I have. Maybe our best has already been done and we failed to notice." She smiled and shrugged. "Or maybe not."

It was true, he thought. There were few plausible grand gestures. Mostly life was small though decisive events, one after another, one minute decision leading by a hidden, connecting path to the next, which would also be minute and probably not especially memorable. By the end of a life a person would have done the best they could do many times, countless times. Though you could isolate these moments and see them as separate, they were a seamlessness which never stopped moving. And this seamlessness encompassed the lives of the others, and it kept moving, flowing on.

They walked down the concourse through the muted canticle of thousands of voices. Clayton imagined how the crowd they were part of would look from above. Like the swaying sea, he thought. Or like a single wave, as it moves through water, rocking itself at the same time that it rocks the water it moves through.

THE GIRLS OF FORTRESS AMERICA

1

"Fortress America, that's what Taft calls it," my father said. His buddy Voneda tapped a Camel out of his pack, then struck a match on his thumbnail. It was May of my eleventh year in the world. I had a loose but definitive sense of things unseen. Air was a teeming, the million events of breath. I was still so soft I took the impression of whatever pressed against me.

I'd begged off going to First Lutheran with my mother because I wanted to stay home with my father. No matter that men's conversation was pistons and points, the price of gas and batting averages. I lusted for the swagger and muscle of their talk. I was pleased he'd brought up Senator Taft. It would give me a chance to ask about fallout.

I was an ignoramus. In Social Studies, Brownowski's discourse on World War II droned on, and my mind would slip out, like a stick shift slipping out of gear, and there I'd be, riding a sleek, red mare through long grass. Actually, I seldom got to ride a horse, but in my imagination I was intimate with the sheen of coats and long tails lashing out and flicking off flies, their great horse nostrils and flighty eyes. Often I pretended I was a palomino mare like the one Dale

Evans rode, or a wild pony Indians would like to capture. Sometimes I fancied myself the black stallion, snorting, pawing at the earth with my hoof.

I knew we were the inventors of the atom bomb, and I knew the atom bomb had smashed a whole city of Japanese at one blow. But I'd missed a step. I did not associate the bomb with fallout. It was the era of the Red Scare, and the way I understood it, it was the Russians who'd invented fallout. Any day now, people thought, the Russians would fly over and sprinkle their arsenic on Kansas City and across the fields, a kind of deadly crop dusting. Would it eat up the soles of our feet? Should I stop going barefoot? Would it eat holes in our voices while we slept?

In fifth grade I'd asked my father if fallout could hurt us.

"Washes down the drain," he'd said. "Gone with the first rain." He was Larry Boyer, owner of the franchise Boyer Chevrolet. His Distinguished Service Cross lay in its satin lined box on top of the chest of drawers in my parents' bedroom. Who was I to doubt a hero?

"How long does fallout last?" I'd asked.

"Take it easy, Sweetheart," he'd said. "Don't you worry about a thing like that."

Now he motioned with his hand. He was going to educate me. He liked to remind me America was Number One. We had Henry Ford, Babe Ruth, Marilyn Monroe, and John Wayne. This country was the greatest country in the world. Our vacations were trips to the Garden of the Gods, Old Faithful, the Alamo. My mother commandeered other tourists to snap the three of us beside geysers or statues of generals on horseback, and my father read the inscriptions on monuments aloud. Brave men had battled their way west, clearing Indians out of the path of pioneer damsels. Now Fortress America, the next step in our westward progress.

"Come over here," he said. He took down the atlas and opened it to the Western Hemisphere. "Taft says it's this long rectangle, from the North Pole down to the tip of South America." He traced an invisible border with his finger." We dig in, hold that line all around the edge."

"It's to keep somebody out?" I said.

"Right you are," Voneda said. "The commies and their fluoridation."

"That's the stuff in our milk?"

"Nope," Voneda said. "You're thinking of radiation. Fluoridation, that's in the water. It's radiation gets in the milk."

"Fallout, honey," my father said. "He means fallout."

"Yep," Voneda said. "That's why the Nesbitts built that cement thing. A fallout shelter they call it."

Ed Nesbitt worked for the post office. Fat Marlene, his daughter, was in my class. Only her mother was thin. They lived two houses away, but I played with Marlene only when I was desperate. Her belly, like her father's, sagged over the elastic band of her shorts. Her fat scared me. Grace Kelly and Audrey Hepburn were the movers and shakers, and they did not carry excess blubber. Also I believed fat was linked by genetics with stupidity. If you were fat, you were dumb and weak. Marlene was a loser. Worse, she liked me.

My father walked to the fireplace, then turned to face us. "This country's the greatest country in the world and it's going to stay that way."

"Yessir!" Voneda said, slamming his fist down on my mother's Danish Modern coffee table.

Heat rose in waves from the pavement. In the elm the turtledoves' babies had hatched. The mother flew up with a worm in her beak.

"Taft is a smart man," my father said.

"Darn right," Voneda responded. He ground out his stub in the ashtay and stood up. "Well," he said. "Got to get back to the wife."

The cowboys and the indians, the fox and the geese, Russia and America. In such an atmosphere a fallout shelter seemed mere prudence. Governor Rockefeller was promoting a luxury model with a ranch style rec room, a bar and barstools. I was fascinated by a couple in Florida who'd spent their honeymoon in their new shelter. Recorded by *LIFE* magazine photographers, they'd descended, carrying a bottle of champagne and two crystal glasses. When they emerged two weeks later, they talked as though they'd been in Tahiti. The wife wore an off-the-shoulder sundress. Her lips in the black and white photo were dark, shiny. I imagined her lipstick, Desert Siren. The husband had one arm around her shoulders. With his other hand he signaled thumbs up.

The Nesbitt's fallout shelter was just one of the imbecile things in their yard. There was a concrete darky holding a light bulb, an imitation rococo style birdbath made of concrete, a concrete Tree of Knowledge with a snake twining up its trunk, and a concrete whale from whose maw Jonah rushed out in terror. When I played horse, I trotted through these furnishings, then cantered off into the unobstructed prairie of my father's lawn.

The Nesbitts had dug a great hole, ruining their yard. I could not approve the destruction of grass. The deep ground seemed a sacred and inviolable privacy. When my mother and I turned it over with a trowel it fluffed up and lay there looking rich and prosperous. You could tell it liked being handled and turned at the surface, little bits at a time.

But the Nesbitts had dug down, violating the secret places. The shelter lacked style. To make it more interesting I decided it resembled an Egyptian tomb. I stocked it with artifacts: the king's crown, barrels of emeralds. A poisonous snake, coiled in a basket, guarded the queen's diamond.

Then my father's chapter of the Masonic Lodge began holding its meetings there. Secret meetings, where women weren't allowed.

"I think it's mean of them to keep secrets," Judy said. The Monopoly board lay between us. Westward expansion was still in progress. We were in training to become developers.

I relied on Judy to keep me informed. When I forgot to clip a current event for Social Studies, she'd have two and give me one. Where I was foggy, she had definition. Where I was hopeful, she was a wrecking ball. I liked to dawdle, and she was the fastest runner in our class. When we played horses, she wanted to be the white one strutting at the head of things. I preferred the mystery and witchiness of dark things. In darkness you could be angry, with tangled hair and ash smeared across your forehead.

"My mother says the men drink beer and play cards," I said. She worked for Elgin's, a jeweler. It was a world where untidy facts did not enter. Every morning she put on her girdle and dressed to the hilt. Though she was slender, the girdle was part of her chosen apparatus. It was the Age of Containment. In a girdle she would never act rashly.

I knew men liked to conceive heroic acts. And I bought my father's notion of the fragile damsel. I believed I needed saving. At Bible School that spring I'd thrown myself at Christ like a hussy. I'd been saved the year before, and salvation had been electrifying. I longed to be zapped once more by its current.

"Maybe they're planning a way to save us," I said. "Maybe they'll save us from a tornado."

"They can't save fish from drowning," Judy said. "They're plodders. What they want to do is slow everyone else down too. *That's* what they're probably planning. How to slow down all fast-moving things."

"Why would they want to do that?"

"Sandra, you're such a dumbbell. So nobody can get there ahead of them. They like to be first."

"It's boys who want to be first. Men are polite. They open doors for women and let them go through."

"That's just show. It doesn't mean anything. Besides, women were slowed down a long time ago, when they were girls."

What would a slowed-down girl look like? Like Marlene, I thought. Cooper, the track coach, made her run like the rest of us, but she came in last, panting. She could not toss her head in triumph, showing off her glorious mane. Fat was a casing inside which she was a prisoner. I despised her for agreeing to such diminished circumstances.

I intended to become great. I toyed with the idea of running for president. I had failed to notice that former presidents of the United States have been men. In my mind they were simply presidents, a cateory unto itself. They were like the pole vaulters, the shot putters, the basketball players. We had Alexander Graham Bell, and George Washington Carver who invented over one hundred uses for the peanut. I intended to pull myself up by my bootstraps. Carver had done it. Lincoln had done it. I would do it.

I knew if I wanted to govern, I'd need to know history. I'd picked the Russians as the topic for my Social Studies

report. I imagined this topic would get my father's attention, and my research would clarify why the Russians had
decided to ruin the world. I would look up facts in
an encyclopedia, write these down in orderly paragraphs,
and presto! I would feel knowledge in the deep muscles of
my being.

But I opened the encyclopedia against the backdrop of
America's fear of the Bear. Later Ike's granddaughter would
marry a Soviet space scientist and advisor to Gorbachev, but
in 1951 we held the Russians responsible for cancer, the
common cold. The encyclopedia corroborated America's
view that Russia was a peasant nation where women wore
kerchiefs and men failed to speak in complete sentences. I
imagined their talk as a series of exclamations. "Eat! Drink!"
they called out, wiping their mouths on their sleeves.
"Soviet!" they shouted. "Five Year Plan!" If weather was the
topic, they'd address it the same way. "Blizzard! Ice storm!
Thaw! Tulips!"

Photographs showed men maneuvering huge timbers
lashed together down the Volga. Stevedores unloaded ships
at Vladivostok. Peasants threshed grain by hand, and women
stepped into harness and pulled plows through rocky fields.
The leaders were a few ruthless men at the top. Their jaws
had been selected out for squareness.

"What about fallout?" I asked Brownowski.

He looked at me critically. Help would not develop self-
reliant citizens. "What did I tell you? What did I say about
sources?"

There was nothing to do but leave out the part about
fallout. To clinch things I copied out the lineage of all forty-
two Tzars beginning with Alexander Nevsky, Son of Prince
Yaroslav II, going all the way down to Nicholas II, son of
Alexander III. Brownowski would admire this compendium

of the rich and powerful, and it summed up the nature of the Russian nation as I understood it. The Tzars were a cold-blooded bunch, and the unrelenting fact of their names in a row implied, I thought, why the Russians had thought up fallout: brutes will be brutes.

"Maybe we could get Marlene to listen in on one of their meetings," I said. Judy and I walked home at dusk, the glory of Coke fizzing in our stomachs. The day before I'd resolved to break into the shelter. Breaking and entering was crime, but wasn't the men's exclusiveness the first crime?

When I told Judy I hoped to run for the presidency, she shook her head.

"Not a chance. You have to be a man."

"Is that in the Constitution?"

She shrugged. "There's never been a woman president."

Later I looked in the encyclopedia: nearly two centuries, and there had not been a single woman.

I'd sneaked over to the Nesbitt's when Edna and Marlene were gone, but I was disappointed: the shelter door was iron. Embedded in it was a lock not even a genius could pick.

"We get her to listen in, then tell us," I said.

"They'll never let her. They won't even let in Edna."

"I can't stand Marlene," I said. "She's such a pig."

"She got that fat from her stupid father."

"The father pig," I said. We were coming up the alley past the hollyhocks. As a little girl I'd turned the blossoms upside down to make dancing girls. Sycamore leaves became gondolas ferrying these damsels across our goldfish pool for a night of revelry with princes. Now I imagined Fortress America, a castle surrounded by a moat. At the hollyhocks' ball the dancing stops. It has begun to snow, the finest flakes. The dancers look up. Slowly the horror dawns on them.

The men had gathered in the Nesbitts' yard for their Lodge meeting. Ed had erected a flagpole on top of the shelter. Every morning he raised the Stars and Stripes, and every evening he lowered them. Now one of the brothers blew some notes on a bugle. They stood at attention, American Gothic, and began to recite the Pledge of Allegiance.

I was enamored of the pledge, that magic incantation of Democracy. It belonged to rich and poor, young and old, women and men, Democrats and Republicans. *With liberty and justice for all*. It was holy writ. Ed climbed the mound, unhooked the guideline and brought the flag down. When he'd climbed down, my father stepped forward. Together they folded the flag in precise, timed movements. The others saluted. Then my father and Ed saluted each other.

"What a lot of crap,"

I was impatient with her. She liked to disparage men. I wanted their power. I left her and walked boldly up to Ed.

"Can I see your Purple Heart?"

"Sandra," my father said, "We're having a meeting."

"Edna's got it in there on the shelf," Ed said.

"Could you take us in and show us?"

"Sandra! This is not the time!" my father said. "Run along."

We ran along. In my defense, Judy produced some thrilling gore.

"You know what happens after fallout? First your hair falls off. You push it behind your ear and there it is in your hand. You start to brush it and instead of staying there like it's supposed to, it comes out in the brush. All of it."

"Your hair will grow back later."

"It *doesn't* grow back. You're a bald girl from then on."

"You could wear a wig."

"You could. For a while. But you die soon after so it doesn't much matter. Besides, you're throwing up. You don't feel like getting dressed up and putting on a wig."

"This talk is driving me nuts," I said.

"I might go crazy too," Judy said. "I might start screaming someday and cross my eyes and not be able to stop."

I contemplated this.

"Another thing you might not know," she said. "Fallout is not a passing fancy. Fallout lasts four million years."

In spite of the fact that I'd failed to find out why the Russians had invented fallout, I'd been stamped with an A, Brownowski's *Good Housekeeping* Seal of Approval. When my father came home from Boyer Chevrolet, I went to him.

"Here," I said, "look."

"'The Russian People,'" my father said. In his mouth my subject sounded like material for the Nobel Prize. Then he looked at me. "Why this sudden interest in the Reds?"

"Brownowski assigned us each a country," I lied.

"I see," he said frowning. "Well, you've done a fine job. Congratulations, sweetheart." He held out the manuscript. He looked as though he just might have a word with this teacher.

"Don't you want to read it?" I asked.

"You got an A, sweetheart," he said. "That's good enough for me. We'll have some ice cream later, to celebrate."

He stood up then, and I followed him out to the Chevy. I was titillated by the glamor of those hulking machines, especially the brand new cars in his showroom. I associated them with my father. They matched his shiny attractiveness.

Beneath his gleaming exterior surely there was cushioned plush, a humming motor.

He opened the hood and pulled up the dipstick. I loved his fingernails, his hair. I loved his bones, holding this body upright. His fatigue jacket, his basketball, his hat, and his head without a hat. I loved his car, because it was his. He loves his car, I too love his car. His windshield scraper, his lug wrench, his glove compartment where he let me keep a roll of LifeSavers for the open road.

I stood beside him, looking into the mystery of the engine.

"How does lubrication work?" I said. I'd given him an opening. Now he could instruct me. Instead he looked stupefied.

"You put some grease on some parts, they move," he said. "You oil things, they run."

"Does the Lodge have a mascot?" I said.

"Sweetheart, I can't divulge that information," he said. He slid the dipstick back in, then stood and closed the hood. At that moment he displayed the impenetratbility of a Sherman tank.

"You can tell about the mascot because it isn't impor-tant."

"You're wrong there," he said. "When you take a vow of secrecy, you swear. You can't go back on your word."

I looked for a glint of amusement in his eyes. There wasn't any. some people could have special privileges and others could not, this is just how things are. I was wild with jealousy.

The baby turtledoves had grown and flown. Now the body of the mother lay at the base of the elm. A bumblebee or two nosed about. Amidst this doze the dove's stillness was electrifying.

I'd been keeping an eye on things, and the evidence was not good. On the leaves of the elms I'd detected a white film. Sometimes there were specks in the mud beneath the spigot, as though someone had spilled powdered sugar.

"Flaking paint," my father had said. I didn't believe him.

Now I marched into the kitchen, a cortege of one. My mother was washing the breakfast dishes. My father stood, drinking the last of his coffee.

"Look," I said. I held out the bird. "Fallout."

"Do you want a shoe box for that bird?" my mother said.

"This bird was fine yesterday," I said.

"It probably just died," my mother said.

"They don't just die," I said. "Something makes it happen."

"Death," she said.

"Got to get to work," my father announced. He went out whistling. On his showroom floor there was a convertible on one side and on the opposite side, a sedan. You could be flashy or sedate. Daring or cautious. Either way it was Chevrolet.

Was I freedom's only defender? I determined then to dance a magic dance against fallout. Exorcism was what I had in mind, ceremonial and final.

"Can I have that pot?"

"Why not." My mother was phasing out the cast iron, phasing in the copper-bottom stainless steel. She'd long ago given me her black crepe dress, and I went up to my room and put it on. Then I took the pot out to the alley, tied three sticks together, and suspended the pot from this tripod. Into it I tossed a handful of bottle caps, some bent tin can lids, rusty nails, a piece of soap, crushed leaves from the elm trees, a feather from the dove's wing. I added water and dirt for binder.

While this poison cooked, I danced around the pot, chanting. *Earth, sun, earth, sun.* I would dance and chant the ground safe for democracy. I would throw my power up with such force that fallout would not dare come down.

It was then that Marlene came shuffling down the alley. Ever since the men had begun to hold their Lodge meetings in the shelter, I'd been zeroing in on Marlene. The name Nesbitt made me think of Alexander Nevsky. For all I knew the Nesbitts could actually be Russians. Marlene resembled those women pulling plows through rocky fields. Grace Kelly and Audrey Hepburn sustained themselves with cucumber sandwiches and salad with a hint of dressing. Marlene lived to down one cinnamon roll after another.

She was proof that girls could be slowed down to practically zero. That morning she wore a dress with belt loops but no belt. There was powdered sugar on the end of her nose.

"What are you doing?" she asked.

"Magic," I said. "I'm doing magic."

"Make me thin then. I want to be popular."

I had not expected the nakedness of her plea. It was as though a little door in front of Marlene's heart had opened, revealing her longing in naked detail. I was amazed, and thrilled, and then, zoom, I began to plot. I didn't hesitate more than a couple of seconds.

"I can make your fat invisible, but you'll never make cheerleader. I can do magic but I can't work miracles."

"Try!" she said.

"Okay. But you can't cry. And you can't say anything until I say you can. Now get down on your knees and say please." I was lead. She knelt on the sharp stones.

"Please."

"All right," I said. "Stand up." I dipped my hand into the pot. "Your cheeks are too fat," I said. "We'll have to get rid of that." I smeared goo on both sides of her face, on the folds of her neck, and on her arms and hands and fingers. I rubbed my poison on her feet and legs. She stood there, muddy and desolate. I was aware that I dared not feel sympathy for her or my enterprise would collapse. I took the stick and began to chant.

"Fat face, fat cheeks, fat neck, fat neck,

Fat arm, fat leg, fat pig, fat pig."

Each time I said the word fat I whacked her lightly with the stick. There were tears in her eyes, but she did not make a sound. I kept it up, chanting and whacking, until I had built up my nerve to a high pitch.

"Fat legs, fat legs, fat feet, fat feet,

Stupid stupid fat pig, here's some fat for you to eat!"

I tried to push the stick between her teeth, but it fell out. I stepped back. The slump of her shoulders seemed unutterably sad. She was trying hard not to cry. I began to feel a little sick.

"You can go now," I said. She turned away and stumbled off, sobbing little wisps of sobs. They were shocking, these cries of hers, each one a faltering ranging up and down the scale, a quavering warble.

I stood there, taking in the fact of what I'd done, and a runnel of fear swept across me like wind riffling water. Then, as I watched, a single hollyhock blossom fell onto those sharp stones at my feet, and lay there on its side, still.

2

That autumn the leaves came down like rain. First one, an accident adrift on the air. Then one more, spiraling, the air cooler, then four and five at a time, leaves by the handful. Down they came, blowing across sandlots and streets, gathering along curbs, in the corners of porches. The wind nattered amidst them, a moan. They clattered dryly against each other.

I'd spent the summer plagued by guilt. I'd be splashing in turquoise water at the swimming pool, feeling fine. Then I'd remember what I'd done to Marlene, and there I'd be amidst the wreckage of a bombed landscape littered with the bodies of slaughtered horses. What I'd done had backfired. It was as though I'd coated myself with mud and defilement. Even turquoise water could not wash the shame off.

I knew I ought to apologize. But apology, next to the bulk of my crime, seemed insufficient. Absolution was what I needed. But to whom could I confess? I longed for a priest, hidden behind a screen. But we were Lutheran.

My mother had noticed. "Don't you want to come with me to church today?" she asked. I'd watched her getting into her girdle. I'd tried one on once, and it felt like I was the center of a pour of concrete that was beginning to set up.

Now it was nearly November. I walked home, shivering in my sweater. Every day I left Judy at her corner, then passed the Nesbitt's darky, smiling like a lacky, holding that lightbulb. Suddenly I couldn't stand it any longer. I screwed up what courage I had, climbed their steps, and knocked. Marlene flung open the door.

"I'm sorry for what I did in the alley."

Marlene looked at me a long minute.

"If you want to see the shelter, come on."

I couldn't believe my good fortune. "Your Mom won't mind?"

"She's ironing. She's got a ton of ironing."

I could almost feel the gold ingots in my hands. Marlene took a key from a hook inside the door, and marched off. I walked behind her, keeping a low profile. The shelter's light switch was outside the door. She flipped it on and we went down.

It was a Cadillac of cellars. The Nesbitts had paneled the walls with knotty pine, and above a fake fireplace hung the head of an elk. Two leather recliners faced this tableau, and Edna had folded a plaid hunting blanket over the arm of the one that was Ed's. Between the recliners lay the hide of a grizzly, its claws reaching for the four corners. It had a squashed look, as though crushed by some weight falling straight from above.

When a Chinese emperor died it was the custom to put his wives and concubines in the tomb with him, alive. I imagined Ed's fellow Lodge members bearing his bulk down, laying it out on the bear rug. Then they'd drag down Edna. Only Marlene might get to go free so she could carry on the Nesbitt line.

"If an attack comes," Marlene said, "the wiring will go. We'll have to use candles."

There was a little gas stove that kept the canned goods Edna had stockpiled from freezing. Outside I heard a dog bark, a boy's voice answering. It was wrong to be down here, I thought. We shouldn't dig into mineral sleep, tampering with a plan that had been in place for millions of years.

"You can't see any stars down here," I said.

"Who cares," Marlene said. "You can live without stars."

"That's crazy. Without stars you die."

"Not me," Marlene said. "I could live down here easy."

I decided she probably could. She would live off her fat.

Just inside the door hung a chart, two columns of numbers. The numbers on the right told you how many days to stay inside the shelter for the corresponding amount of fall-out shown on the left. Between the columns stood a woman wearing a tailored suit, a white blouse and khaki tam. Her right hand pointed toward one column, her left toward the other. She was blonde with terrific teeth, Doris Day as a WAC.

Above the door Ed had hung a printed sign: BETTER DEAD THAN RED. Beside the door stood a pick and shovel.

"What are those for?" I asked.

"For digging out, stupid," Marlene said. "For digging out after the blast."

I took in this information. Marlene laughed. Very quickly then she dashed up and out and slammed the door. I registered the sound of that iron door seating in its casement. I heard the key, that clear, dependable turnover and fit of a bolt in a lock that cannot be jimmied. Then the light went out.

The dark was total. There wasn't a crack in it anywhere. I made my way toward where I thought the recliners were, got hold of the hunting blanket, wrapped myself and collapsed into the recliner. I did not question Marlene's act. It was clear that I fit this event the way that bolt had sunk perfectly into its lock. Marlene was getting justice. I was her justice.

I thought of those Chinese women, flanked by a suitable collection of jade, made to lie down in their silks beside a dead man. I had no silks, and I'd been spared the dead man, but the Nesbitts had provided the correct American artifacts: two recliners, a bear rug, and the sliced off head of an elk. All I lacked for the long journey through the ages was a hamburger and some potato salad.

Would I languish here until the next Lodge meeting? Three days! I thought of Jonah in the belly of the whale. If I could make it, *LIFE* might put me on their cover: KANSAS

CITY GIRL SURVIVES PRISONER OF WAR ORDEAL. I imagined being photographed rising out of the ground like Lazarus. It would be good if I'd had some Desert Siren lipstick for the occasion.

Then I was weeping. It was as though I'd reached through space to the dark side, and when I'd pulled back my hand some of the dark had come with it, and now I couldn't get this dark off me, and it kept at me, like something wild clawing my arm.

I slid out of the recliner, still wound in the blanket, and lay down, belly up, on the bear rug. Then I threw open the blanket, as though to bare myself to the elements. Above me was the biggest darkness there is, was, and ever will be. I lay there, and in perfect acquiescence I thought, *let the Russians go ahead and drop their bomb now*. I was penitent and ready to pay.

I was awakened by the sound of that iron door rolled open. Against the night sky I saw Marlene's silhouette in the doorway, holding a flashlight. "Hurry up!" she hissed. "Get out of there!"

The dried skin of blanket fell away. Then I was up the steps, in the open air. There was no moon, but there were stars. In their faint light I couldn't see Marlene's face, but I knew inside her were the most exquisitely filigreed cries.

"Don't you dare tell," she said.

"What time is it?"

"It's practically morning. I called your mother and told her you were spending the night."

"I've never spent the night at your house."

"Your mother thought it was a fine idea."

"What's your mother making for breakfast?" I said.

"We've got cinnamon rolls. And when she gets up she'll make scrambled eggs and cocoa." Marlene paused. "If you're hungry right now, I saved you some peach pie."

"Where is it?"

"I hid it in my room. Come on."

I had risen from the dead. In celebration I got out my watercolors. Color was entrance into the alternative universe. Wasn't I invocation and benediction, psalm and hymn? I began to paint my self-portrait. I was naked, but between my thighs I brushed in a bouquet: poppy and daisy, tulip, peony, rose. Where my breasts would be, two fish swam toward each other, their mouths open. My hair was long and flowing, and on one shoulder a small leopard lay basking. On the other a hummingbird stretched its throat, tasting nectar from a dangling blossom. And in each of my hands I painted a perched bird, ready to swoop off.

Through that winter I did the dishes for my mother without complaining. What had been a burden seemed an opportunity to do her a favor. I understood that Marlene and I shared the kinship of having pulled off crimes of brilliant proportions. I respected her grudgingly for what she'd done to me. It showed she wasn't pablum.

One day when Judy stayed home from school sick, I had no one to walk home with. Marlene had a packed look that day, like she'd stuffed herself the way you stuff a doll with cotton batting.

"Do you want to walk home?" I said.

"Sure." We gathered our notebooks and mittens. She lumbered along beside me, toasty inside her overcoat of fat.

"Maybe the Russians will stop making their bombs and fallout won't fall," I said. "But you can't tell about men. They're not very bright. They could start another war any minute."

"And then kaboom," Marlene said. "We'll go in our shelter. You should get your dad to build one."

"He's going to," I lied. "Next summer."

"I want to fly one of the planes that drops fallout."

"Why? Why do you want to drop fire on people?"

She shrugged. "It's what you do if you're a bomber pilot."

"You'll feel rotten later, after they print pictures of the burned people," I said. "You'll have terrible dreams."

"Not me," Marlene said. "I don't dream."

"Dropping fallout isn't to your advantage," I said. "It blows around in the wind. The fallout you drop is going to make you sick too, along with the Russians."

"That's what shelters are for," Marlene said. "You go in and rest a while. Then fallout's gone, and you come out."

"You're wrong," I said. "It lasts four million years."

"That just proves we're the best inventors in the world."

"We didn't invent fallout," I said. "The Russians did."

"Boy are you dumb," Marlene said. "We dropped the first atom bomb in the world, and from that whopper the first fallout fell."

Instinctively I knew she had to be right. All this time I'd thought I was getting smart, I had remained an ignoramus.

"Anyway," I said, "if you want to drop fallout, you have to be in the air force, and you can't be."

"I can too. I'm going to join the WACs."

"Marlene," I said, "this is wishful thinking. They won't give a WAC a bomb to drop."

"Why not?"

"Because they think women are nervous and flighty. They think you'll miss the target."

"We'd be part of the air force. They'd have to let us bomb."

I shook my head. "Never in four million years. You're a girl. Listen," I said. "Did your parents change the family name from Nevsky to Nesbitt? If it's a secret, I promise not to tell."

Marlene looked blank. "What kind of name is that?"

"It's Russian," I said. "Ask your dad. Maybe your grandparents did it."

"My dad hates Russians," she said.

There's a way both the ground and the air seem to swell in April, as though saturated with liquid becoming. Then there are warm days, and the earth begins to dry out. Birds move in with their baggage. The air made me think of ads for Johnson's Baby Powder. There were pale new leaves, and grass.

The daffodils bloomed, and so did my breasts. I was resurrection: adults would have to pay attention. I'd get a driver's license. I'd open a checking account. Also, I intended to enter the arena of romance. The powerful feelings I was experiencing I'd seen at the movies—Ava Gardner and Elizabeth Taylor had them. Lauren Bacall had them. I was fascinated by the way these women inhabited their bodies. I envisioned myself sweeping across ballrooms where boys fell back against the wall, struck with desire as though by lightning. Or I was Calamity Jane on horseback, going after bandits, pursued by cowboys so handsome I could scarcely stay on my feet in their presence.

I would not let Marlene's callous views faze me. And now my father would spill the secrets of the Lodge. He'd slip me the keys to power: how you got it, how you used it, how you kept it coming. He'd take me wherever he went, show me off, help me plan a fabulous future as an explorer or someone like Henry Ford bringing stunning new inventions into being.

One evening I found him reading the paper. I sat beside him, leaned over his print, began to read. Burglars had used the woman's own handbag to carry off her diamonds.

"What's this about a robbery?" I said.

"Sandra, you're practically on top of me. What do you want?"

Everything, I thought. "Nothing," I said.

"Do you need a ride somewhere?"

It distressed me that a ride in his car was still the only favor it occurred to him to bestow. He seemed not to notice my new dispensation, and this irked me. But I did not want to feel disappointed. I gathered my own presence around me. "I'm just sitting here," I said. "It's a free country."

My father did not give me the satisfaction of a reply. Now it seems an index of how pleased I was with my new powers that on this occasion I decided not to feel rejected but triumphant. Good, I thought, when he ignored me. Good. I've reduced him to silence.

I had gone to the library to browse amidst reproductions of the masters. I hoped to pick up tips on becoming a master myself. I leafed through the largest book I could find. There I came upon Goya's *Fight with Cudgels*. In Goya's painting, human interaction has been reduced to the head-on face-off of hand-to-hand combat. Two men, muscular in a solid uncompromising way, face each other. Their expressions are stripped of civilizing grace, and the cudgels resemble roughly-hewn and thickened baseball bats. The men have pulled back, ready to swing, and their eyes are large with the exigency of the moment. Each body is braced to deliver a murderous blow and to receive the blow of the other. The landscape is unrelieved by even a single bit of foliage. The sky threatens a rolling storm, and in the center of this sky appears a panel of light. But this light is momentary and dwindling. It will be enough to see by to deliver the blows. Then it will go out.

I thought of the photo I'd seen in *LIFE* magazine of two tanks—one Russian, one American. They were so similar they might have been constructed by the same manufacturer. Each tank filled its page. There was no backdrop, no foreground. Landscape had been obliterated by hardware. There was no sky.

There was US and there was THEM. Everywhere you looked we'd been sliced in half. I'd taped to the wall of my room a photograph of a sculpture. The sculptor had begun with a thick block of white stone. Now this block was a face cracked down the middle, its eyes crossed. Where the mouth should have been was a gag, a white stone bandage. The face was so hurt you couldn't tell if it was a man or a woman.

I'd tacked it up beside a shot of Doris Day from *Photoplay*. She looked like a doll stood up beside a concentration camp survivor. Which would win?

I walked home from the library, pondering the ways of mankind. In my room I'd studied the face more closely. All of a sudden my perception did one of those perspective flips, and I saw it wasn't a face at all. It was two figures in profile, slapped together. I looked at the fine print beneath the photo. *The Kiss,* it said, by Brancusi.

The kissers were blocky halves of a rectangle. What I'd thought was a gag was a strip of binding crushing them against each other. I imagined an angry god picking up one in each hand, slamming them together. Just as the two tanks would bang together to the end, it was the fate of these kissers to kiss to infinity.

"Do you want another Coke?"

Judy shook her head. We lolled on my mother's new porch couch. This couch was the site of a gathering of jungle blossoms, suggesting we'd made our escape to the tropics and now lounged amidst the splendor of voluminous growth. I imagined us reclining in white dresses, each sipping a drink with a name like Mai Tai, prettified by a slice of pineapple.

"I found this picture," Judy said. "In a magazine."

"What picture?" Since my conversation with Marlene I'd been armoring myself with skepticism. When giddy excitement arose, I was a glass of ice water. On the other hand, Judy had once shown me a magazine with a picture of a man and woman kissing. The woman's shoulder strap had slipped off and her dress looked about to fall. I hoped the picture was another of these.

"It was this horse," Judy said. "This was at Hiroshima."

I can still hear her voice, her delivery a little too fast, and myself, in response, a little too shrill.

"So?" I said.

"This horse is all by itself, standing on flat ruin. Not a tree or a bush or a house. Everything's burned all the way up."

"How can a horse be there if everything else is gone?"

"People and animals didn't know where they were going. They were too shocked to think straight. The place was one big ruin."

"And right there suddenly appears this perfectly good horse," I said.

"No," she said. "It's a wrecked horse. It's alive and standing up, but it's got no skin on. A complete, standing horse, but its hide has burned off."

Horses, to my mind, seemed superior. There was marvelousness and a mystery about them people didn't possess, and they did not do stupid, unnecessary things.

"Where its ears should be are just little bumps."

"That's not true!" I said. "It's impossible for a horse to stand up without skin!"

"Its hooves were perfectly all right, but because the skin's gone you can see the veins and arteries all over it. It's just standing there like it can't move, looking out."

"Who took this picture?" I shouted. "No one could take that picture! Somebody made it up just to scare people. Nobody around there would have a camera."

"Maybe some Americans came in with cameras."

"That's nuts!" I shouted. "Americans aren't crazy. They'd get as far away from that thing as they could."

"They didn't know much then," Judy said. "People weren't very bright."

I wished I had something to wrap around me, a quilt of the sort that appear in fairy tales which neither weather nor disaster can penetrate. "That horse would have died right away," I said.

"Yes," Judy said. "But for a few minutes it was just standing there, perfectly alive."

Judy sat up. "I should go home," she said. "My dad promised to show me how to make a tourniquet."

At that moment my father came out, dangling his keys. His handsomeness still surprised me. Gullible women, I thought, would ask for his autograph.

"Where are you going?" I said.

"To the hardware store."

"Take us with you," I said.

"Sandra, you know you don't want to go there," he said.

Suddenly the clink of nails in bins, the shininess of nuts waiting for the fit of a bolt, the mysterious uses metal could be put to—washers, lengths of pipe, wire—all these engaged me. Judy was going to be taught to tie a tourniquet, and I wanted to be shown the world of hardware by my father. I wanted to appreciate the utility of shovels, the intricacy of electrical sockets. Men put their hands on these things, they used them. It was reason enough.

"Please!" I said.

"This is just one of your wild ideas," my father said. "You'll get bored and be needling me to take you home. If you want a ride somewhere else, I'll drop you off."

I sighed and cast a penetrating gaze into the distance.

"Sandra," he said, "will you make up your mind?"

"Tell us what you do in the Lodge. Are you planning to save the world?"

"Nothing quite that ambitious," he said.

"Tell us *something*," I said. "Anything!"

"Sandra," he said, "you're too much at loose ends. You've been mooning around here batting your eyelashes, and you don't lift a finger to help your mother."

"That's not true!" I said, though it was partly true. I'd been carelessly forgetting my chores now and then, though I hadn't intended to leave my mother in the lurch.

"It's true enough," he said, "but I can't argue now."

I squeezed my eyes shut and listened to his footsteps going down the steps. He knew exactly where he was going. I was painfully aware that such was not my nature. I opened my eyes. The clouds were cottony, ethereal. I studied their shifting shapes, their light-bodied billowing, their swift dreaminess. What I had in mind for myself was

STORIES BY MARILYN KRYSL

a life resembling those clouds. But I lived amidst barbarians. Such frivolity and fluidness, in our hard age, seemed against national principles. The F.B.I., I thought, would not approve of these clouds.

I thought then of the Brancusi, that stone kiss. I wished hard for a way to tear my father from me. But that would have been like ripping off my own skin. He was just in me, chromosomes and mitochondria. There was no way to get his contribution out.

My father went off to the last Lodge meeting of May. My mother sat with me in the living room, looking lovely, sewing a button on a satin blouse. I had homework, but I wanted to look at *LIFE* magazine instead. The Shah of Iran, deposed, looked out from the cover. Inside was an ad for the Natural Rubber Bureau. *Route Nine,* it declared *Starts in Southeast Asia.* The illustrator's tropical landscape was dwarfed by a giant tire.

I paged through to the photo essay. Two chimps wearing tennis dresses swung rackets, lobbing balls hither and yon. I turned the page. *Atomic Open House* the title announced. "Last week," the article began, "like animal trainers ready to show off a monster they have tamed, the men of the AEC exploded an A bomb for the whole U.S. to see." I stared at the photograph. A low hillside in the desert swarmed with photographers and the one hundred and ninety-seven reporters called in to cover this historic event. Amidst sparse sage they looked like gnats.

At the bottom of this hill the AEC had set up bleachers. The bleachers were lined with men wearing goggles with dark lenses. They wore suits, but some had taken off their jackets and rolled up their shirt sleeves. They leaned forward, legs spread, elbows on their knees, intent on the play. Except for those goggles, they looked like this was an ordinary Sunday at the ball park. At any moment a girl in a short skirt might walk by selling Coke and hot dogs.

My mother finished securing the button, snipped the thread, then threaded the needle again. She kept herself firmly but prettily away from warfare. Crudeness, when she was forced to recognize it, was a blight across her personal time.

And my father? He would throw up some bluster about Taft, or assert the wisdom of Eisenhower. If I threw four million years at him, his denial would kick in. He would address me as though I were still in primary school: *Sweetheart* this and *Sweetheart* that.

It occurred to me that I was alone in the world. I read on. The goggles, the blurb explained, were to protect the men's eyes from the killing brightness of the blast. But these goggles made the men look like they'd been blindfolded.

When the blast was over, I imagined, the men would take them off and ogle the brunette advertising a girdle on the opposite page. The girdle was rubber with little circles cut out so the woman's skin could breathe. Wearing a bra, this girdle, garters and stockings, the brunette danced through three different ballet positions. Her carefree capering was calculated to make the girdle seem a liberating garment. It was called the New Invisible Playtex Living Girdle. In it you would cause the prince to fall on his knees, slide the glass slipper onto your foot. In it you would never get sick or be tired. In it the bomb would drop, the dead fall down around you, trees and grass give up the ghost, but you would be there, all by yourself, alive. In that girdle you wouldn't feel anything.

3

I dreamed many girls walking single file in a line. Marlene was in the line, and Judy, and the other seventh grade girls, and a third grader I baby-sat, and girls I didn't know, girls and more girls. They walked single file, taking very small steps, their eyes cast down. They walked very, very slowly. The line crept along.

I began to walk in the direction the line was going. I walked until I saw the Nesbitts' house. The line curved around to the back, and there was the shelter. At the door stood Coach Cooper. He held his whistle in his teeth, in case he should need to blow a sharp blast. As each girl arrived, he motioned her in. One by one each girl went down.

I turned away and began to walk in the opposite direction. I passed girls and more girls, but I kept walking away. The line continued until the landscape turned into desert. I crossed sand studded with creosote bushes, expanses bare except for a few rocks. Here and there I saluted a lizard. Now and then I was eyed by a rabbit or a bird.

I walked, still going in the opposite direction of the line. There were little flowers in the sand, and in that great quiet I bent down. Each one had a voice, and I put my ear close. They called out in tiny chorus. *Yes, yes,* they sang. *Yes, yes, go on.*

Then very faintly I heard a low thundering. From out of the distance there came cantering toward us a band of horses. When they reached the line of girls they stopped. There were black horses and white horses, spotted horses, pintos and palominos. All of these horses had great glistening bodies. Their flanks shone with the sweat of their charge.

Without warning a girl peeled off from the line and went toward the horses. Then another girl pulled away, and a third. Then two girls peeled off at once. The girl in back of them paused, and the line behind her slowed, wobbled. The wobble took a whole section of the line with it and fell away.

Every girl there wanted to touch the horses. Every girl there wanted a horse of her own. One girl got another to give her a leg up onto a pinto, swung her leg over and sat, ready to ride. The rest of us followed her example, each going after the horse that seemed to be our own. I found my palomino mare, and with a leg up from the girl next to me, I mounted.

The palomino's back was broad and warm, the way I'd imagined. I was tall, and there were a lot of us. We were many girls, a hoard of girls, an extravagance of girls, a great force of girls. I nudged my horse into a trot, and the others turned their horses to follow me. We began to ride then, going in the direction from which the line had come, toward that faraway land which would keep moving away from us, slowly but steadily, though we longed for it and rode and rode toward it, that beautiful land, that lost world.

Morning in May is a many splendored thing. Sparrows twittered busily. The air smelled sweet. A border of marigolds chorused their unnameable color. The grass looked expensive, like a fur coat.

I went down the stairs. Would I dare to be buoyant? Though it wasn't a matter of daring. It was a matter of knowing too much, not being able not to know. It did something to your ability to float. My father sat at the breakfast table, a cup of coffee before him. Suddenly I couldn't take my eyes off him. He looked smaller than I remembered, and he stooped a little, a thing I'd never noticed. It gave him an air of weariness, something you'd think a man who'd been decorated would not allow.

My mother was even more what she'd always been. She'd dressed for work in a navy blue sheath with a modest little white collar. Though she was discreet about display, she had presence. She wiped the counter with a sponge, looking like a queen sent to the scullery. She did not belong in an ordinary kitchen, but there she was, wiping the counter, married to my father.

I wondered then if the fallout had reached Kansas City yet. Was it even now drifting down invisibly over the toast, the orange juice, the coffee? Was there fallout in my hair? When I brushed my hair did it fly up from the brush, sparks of electricity? Through the window I saw Marlene come out of her house and descend, in nylons and high heels, to the sidewalk. She had a summer job with an accountant, and she looked like she was going off smartly to glory. Head up and belly forward, she went striding past the darky with his light bulb as though he existed merely to witness her departure. Her heels clicked down the sidewalk. The sound reminded me of cash registers. She was a fat girl without refinement, and she was going toward money.

I saw the future in which the barbarians would reign. My mother's Lutheran prayers would not help, nor would my father's senators, or his inventory. When Marlene dropped her bomb, would her brass turn to tin, or would she become a battle ax? Judy might make it through with dignity, becoming a doctor like her father, stitching up the wounded. But I would not fit. Beneath my new, smart self I was still pastel. I just wanted to bask in the sun, watching clouds drift and unravel harmlessly. But I did not live in a nation of baskers.

And there was the danger that I might become one of them. I thought how Judy had told me about the horse, and later I'd gone into the kitchen and peeled potatoes for my mother. People did what they were used to doing, even if it made no sense. They kept at their own destruction. It seemed likely I would do it too.

I knew I had some strengths and some brokenness. The strength of horses to canter long distances without grass or water, to whinny and flick their long tails like soft whips, to rear up on their back legs showing their great bellies, snorting and addressing the surrounding air with their powerful bodies. And then there were many horses battered, burned, and falling down around me, their swift legs useless, their round, wet eyes seeing everything, so many horses and so beautiful, their great massing together falling away, their beauty falling away and away, into destruction.

The truth, the whole truth, and nothing but the truth. That's what they make you swear to tell in court. I went back upstairs and hauled out my self-portrait. Something was missing, and I knew what it was. I got out my watercolors and painted in a pair of glasses. These glasses contrasted with my naked flesh and the flowers and animals that were part of me. They were something outside the natural world, something that set me apart from what I was. They made me see more than I wanted to.

In the background I painted one of those spectacular sunsets the atom bomb made famous. I layered on the rose and gold, playing up this final burst of dying light. In front of this sunset I painted the mushroom cloud, an extravagant explosion centered right behind me. It looks like the bomb is exploding straight up out of my brain.

EATING GOD

They think I fast. They think I stay alive on the infrequent wafer. At evening mass crowds press into our little chapel. They have heard I do not join the sisters at meals, that once I nearly died. They like to think that my miracles are the result of stringent withholding of all nourishment. The idea of starvation thrills them. Saints are known to starve themselves. They want to believe I'm a saint.

They want to believe this because it makes them tingle. They are mesmerized by the idea of suffering. If there is a miracle, it must be paid for. If there is grace, there must be debt. Even a tiny bit of light has, in their scourged minds, a high price. It is what they have been taught, and they have learned to lust for this stern teaching. They bow before the naysaying of high law, its gleaming surface. They give themselves to the beat of its bludgeoning rant.

Rant gives them license to rave, and raving is a passionate act they may allow themselves. How good it feels to fling their upper bodies forward and back, as though they are both beater and beaten, braided hair flying loose, and a mad voice—not theirs—crying out from their parched throats. They rave and relish the thought of me fainting with starvation, the black tunnel opening before me. But in truth I am often a hearty eater. I like a feast of lamb and dumplings, kumquat jelly on thick bread, the filling bulk of squash and pumpkin, the sweet pear, peach, and grape. At times I am so ravenous that my guest is all ascurry to keep me supplied. But those who come come to see a saint who has starved herself.

They do not understand God is in both eating and not eating. He is in the apple my guest brings in the dark, and in the air beside the apple. He is in the bread I eat at midnight and in the world around that bread. Though they do not heed me, I tell them the truth. I say I eat God's body all the time. I say God's body is everywhere, in the air and in the water, in the apple and beside the apple. I open my mouth and God is there, in my mouth. I laugh. I say I am always eating.

In my early days at the convent I did nearly starve myself to death. I began this lunacy by following the hearty suggestions of my advisor. For the archbishop deems it his duty to send the convents these men whose work it is to nurture the purity of female novices. When my advisor spoke I watched his mouth.

—We admire you for the sealed quality of your intact virgin body. In you is no loss of corporeal integrity. But pay heed to shore up any small listing away. Firmly keep your body closed with comely chastity.

—Sir, I shall, I said. For my advisor worked so strenuously at puffing himself up that I felt he needed some little encouragement. And indeed, when I had patted him with a phrase or two, he was much bolstered, and would be moved to more extravagant admonitions.

—Go even to your grave a virgin, he counseled. —For God has given every woman natural closure against man's

STORIES BY MARILYN KRYSL

member, and so He intended you to stay. Therefore keep yourself cleanly shut, all the way to death, where fasting will shortly bring you. Chastity to the death shall be your triumph. Truly you shall have beaten the Devil then, and we shall circle your grave many times with censers and prayers, singing your praise.

—So I shall endeavor, I said, or some such nonsense. For in those days I believed I ought to pay attention to him.

Thus it came about that I determined to give up sustenance. Though the Mother counseled me to defer, I was determined. I consoled the sisters by coming to meals, and tested myself by taking something in my mouth, a bite of bread or a nut or a leaf of salad. I would chew, but when I had done, I would reject this mastication into a small vessel. Afterward I rinsed my mouth with cold water. Thus I stayed undefiled by food.

I reveled in my girlish ripeness for death, in the blandishments of listlessness. And I believed in so doing that I took heroic measures. I would accomplish what no other girl had had the fortitude to bring off. And in due course I weakened greatly. So far down did I sink that the archbishop himself ordered shovelers to dig my grave.

It was winter, the earth beginning to freeze. Still the grave diggers hacked hard ground open. A thin snow fell. When the grave was finished, I wanted to see it. Five of the sisters wrapped me in woolen blankets and carried me out. The most meager of snows had sifted down, and in the center of this flatness dropped my hole. It was exceedingly small, hardly the length of my person. A narrow trench but deep, wherein water might gather if it stormed.

The dirt to be piled on lay handy beside it. Due to lack of nourishment, I had been many hours in dull drowse. Now I came violently awake. Look well, I thought. This is where you are going. On the instant I bade the sisters bear me quickly to my cell. There I said I would take some broth immediately.

—I thought I should lose you, the Mother said. She knelt beside my pallet. —Praise God who has kept you from destruction.

—Praise me, I said. —For I have come to my senses.

She laughed at this, and I called for more broth.

Two nights through I did not sleep. I sipped broth and questioned myself, for it was clear that the near success of my project had required much self-deception on my part. While I recovered, my reputation spread. Many wanted to view my body which had stepped to the dark gate and hung on it, longingly. But where in the past I had relished the attention of these starers, now their goggling struck me with horror. But I did not then have the good sense to disabuse them of their fantasies. Or perhaps I knew how strenuously they would refuse my true story.

From that time on I came religiously to meals. I ate as it suited me, sometimes little, at other times gorging myself. For food is God, and to refuse to eat is to refuse the fleshy sweetness of creation. This, now, I did not want to do.

It was then, when I decided to take on flesh, that my future guest began to take note of me. One day, beside me at table, she reached beneath the board and thrust something into my hand. Afterward, in the hall, I discovered it was a sweetmeat, which I devoured with much relish. She continued to bring me morsels, though she was careful not to let the others see. For we were all to treat each other equally.

My advisor confessed he felt he had failed at his task, that if only he had sufficiently instructed me, I would have persevered to sainthood. He resolved to begin again from the beginning, tutoring me through the many deprivations available to woman.

—I shall instruct you today on the virtue of modesty, he said. —Your purity inspires us, but take care. Your shiny black shoes, by their creaking, give an invitation to young men. For woman is a source of provocation from whom we men must hold ourselves apart, if we are to taste tranquillity. Though comeliness is not to be censured because it is a goodly garment of the soul, still it is to be feared because of the injury and violence it inflicts on men who admire you. So I say to men that even those women who are docile yet need instruction. They must have dress that is quiet, and it must be wrapped and tied securely up, for women are wont to throw off their clothing. To you, Catherine, I would warn that though woman is formed of foul slime, yet you may subdue and chasten those parts of your body that carry men into lust. Wear binding daily over your breasts, and if it gives you comfort, the Mother may purchase for you a belt to keep your nether parts quiet, which only she will keep the key to.

To such nonsense I was forced to listen. Though assiduous care for the closure of my hymen was hardly necessary. I myself adored my shut purse which only I had opened, nor did I want any man but Christ to enter me.

When Christ first came to me, it was the glorious autumn of my eighteenth year. I had been at the nunnery three years, having convinced my father to take me when I was fifteen. I had longed to go there, for I perceived that the sisters gathered to themselves powers of great kindness. They were known to give to anyone who came asking, and the Mother Superior and one or two sisters came and washed and rocked any man or woman who lay dying. There seemed no end to their supply of goodness, and such a supply of largesse was the object of my lust. Kings, clerks, and magistrates had only the power of sternness. No king, clerk, or magistrate had the Mother's lush and abundant base.

And I took as high fashion the Mother's black and white raiment. The black over the white, leaving just a little white showing, to reveal that underneath was all whiteness. It seemed a garment in which to keep delicious secrets. At the same time, it seemed a garment in which to sweep powerfully down corridors lit with torches, arriving at some seat of glowing genius, redolent of the queen's throne. I draped a bed sheet over my head, wrapped myself and swept to where my father sat by the fire.

—It's the Mother Superior herself! he said, and laughed with pleasure at my mimicry.

The Mother Superior was what I hoped to become. My mother had died when I was a baby, and I did not remember her, except her breast where I had sucked with hearty energy. Her absence was made up for by my father, a lover of horses and a maker of carriages. He was kind, and he liked to play and to make me laugh. I loved him and did not want to leave him, but I longed to join those shining women.

When I and my friend began to bleed, I became frightened. She and I liked to make up secrets, and now she was full of whisperings that officials and clergymen sometimes took women aside to question them about foul doings. Further, these churchmen hurt them to make them confess.

Though my father assured me this talk was girls' rumors, it scared me. And then it happened: the mother of my friend was called up for just this questioning! I went to my father and begged him quickly to take me to the convent. He held me close and smoothed my hair, as he liked to do.

—Catherine, he said. —Do not fear. I will protect you. You are too young for the convent, sweetheart, and besides, I cannot yet part with you.

They let my friend's mother go unhurt. But she packed up her family and whisked them off in the dark, not telling anyone where they were going. So fearful were they that my friend was not allowed to tell me good-bye, though she left me a pretty and tearstained note under our secret rock by the stream.

I was disconsolate. Without my friend, each day lacked finery. My father tried to console me, but could not. And thus, being lonely, I threw myself into dreaming of the sisters and the secrets they kept within their habits. Finally, when I reached the age of fifteen, under the onslaught of my pleading, my father let me go.

At eighteen I was still enamored of autumn's leaves. I longed to be like them, turning copper and gold, falling onto the grass. Though it also happened about that time that I was often in a smoldering rage, brought on by my jealousy of those who knew letters. The rule was that monks and priests might get the alphabet, but novices were not to desire it. I had secretly stared at pages of scripture where they lay open on the altar. Each time I felt the words about to fly into me, I would hear footsteps. I would have to walk on, as though I gave not a fig for writing. But secretly I continued to hold myself open, in case words should care to enter me.

On the road back from market one day, I was bending to pick St. John's Wort which we use against melancholia.

There in the road I did get a small book someone had dropped. This was the Bible, and that evening I opened it and looked at the page. One by one the words came straight into me, each one like a match struck, match after match firing my tinder. One word by one word I was reading.

I had opened at random and read some raging of Ezekiel. Now I turned to the beginning. There Eve and her serpent bit deliciously into the apple. Immediately I fell in love with Eve, partly for her daring to eat what she should not, partly that she was the first woman I myself read of. I looked up from the book, imagining her greedy love of fruit, and there—right there—stood Christ. He leaned against the door frame of my cell, a reasonable and ordinary man in a white robe, swathed in the brilliance of lit cloud.

—So you like the apple story?

—Indeed I do, my Lord, I replied.

—You will find even juicier tales in that book, he said, and stories of brave and strong women. But now we must preserve you. For men who hear of your reading will be jealous.

—My advisor will be jealous, I said. —Shall I conceal my new knowledge? For I fear he will forbid me to read.

—Do not give that scoundrel an inch, Christ said. —Declare your gift abroad, and loudly. It will then be taken up by the public as an act of God, and your advisor will not be able to gainsay you.

I fell on my knees, blabbering some gratefulness. For I was now in love with reading. Christ tugged gently and raised me up.

—None of this bowing and scraping, he said. —Quickly now. Announce yourself.

Thus I walked out into the hall with all speed, calling out to my sisters, smashing the glass chalice of prayerful quiet. I strode down the row of cells toward the Mother's quarters, loudly proclaiming the miracle, me.

Next morning the one who would become my guest took my hand beneath the table and slipped into my palm a cake of persimmon. I resolved, when we would enter the hallway after breakfast, to whisper to her. But the Mother entered then and announced that scholars were come to test my reading. I was thrilled that I should perform my miracle in public, but before I might, my advisor swept me away, declaring he must give me warning. For that I had become the vessel of a miracle meant that I must redouble my efforts at chastity.

—It is good for those men who are exceedingly weak and must marry to do so, he said. —Yet I tell them to educate their wives to their proper function. Do not touch the woman, I say, while she bleeds or feeds her child or if she carries another in her belly. Nor during Lent, Advent, nor the Ember days, nor on Sundays, Wednesdays, Fridays, nor Saturdays. Nor for twenty-four hours before communion, should it fall on a Tuesday. Nor on Thursday, in honor of Jesus' arrest.

—But sir, I replied. —If men and women must be separated, how then shall we bring forth more men?

—It will happen more than we would wish it, he said. —But to staunch the flow of men's lust, keep yourself well covered. And in your countenance let there be no expression of any invitation. Do not look at men more than a glance. Then lower your eyes, answer in short phrases. Thus you will take holy pride.

Rich merchants and humble tailors came that morning. Scholars and burghers came, and church fathers in their long robes. My father too came proudly to see me. I was more celebrated than the Resurrection. The archbishop did not come, but sent his representatives to test my reading. When I entered with my Bible, one came and stood beside me. The crowd spilled beyond the doors in tingling silence. This silence I filled.

I read long and well from my Bible and from whatever manuscript a man might hand me. So proud was I to be miraculous that I did not fear to glance up between verses. I looked at these faces, and what I saw astonished me. All my life I had been looking at men's mouths. Except for my father's mouth which was kind with laughter, these mouths I had watched were set in thin, hard lines, or wagged rapidly with ranting fervor. Now, around me, ranged the many mouths of the fathers. And the mouths of the fathers stood open. I looked for the first time into these mouths, and it was as though my reading had taken the words away from them. I saw that those powerful engines were empty. Empty stood their mouths full of silence, empty their sorry mouths of dust.

2

Two years pass before Christ comes again. Now that I read, my day is all the business of the church. I am much in demand, for I am a novelty, a woman denied learning, now gone above the learned. For my part, I inject into my duties licentious pleasure of my own, by which I mean I indulge the thrill of reading to men. I am most brazen. I hold my head high. I pause between verses and look into the eyes of first one man and then another. They glance away, or cast their eyes down.

I spend nights in delicious darkness with my guest. She came to my cell the first time just after I had read myself above the scholars. Because her work is in the pantry, she is able to put aside little dishes. She brings purple plums and goat cheese, a loaf, and a flask of wine. We whisper while we feed each other, and she takes my two hands and kisses them. Then she puts my hands, one on either arm of the chair, and bids me hold tightly. She opens the buttons of my night dress and slowly pulls it back.

My breasts appear in the searing light of the moon. My guest remarks in whispers the opulence of these brooches. Then she lays her palms on my breasts to cool them. I am much taken up with her attentions. And one might suppose that in this suspended state which resembles a kind of heavenly levitation, I would be wont to forget God. But such is not the case. For I know that God is in the apple and beside the apple. He is in the bread and in the air around the bread. There is no escaping His presence. My guest attends me, and I eat God, especially then.

The day Christ pays his second visit I am gathering the rhizomes of the male fern for the sisters to sell at market. These rhizomes are an excellent anthelmintic, but must be used with discretion, for excessive doses may be poisonous. I gather them in the forest, where they are best taken in summer. I do this not solely out of duty, but also for the pleasure of feeling the fern's hairy coil. Before the leaves unfurl, this coil is tight, and my fingers pluck at it deliciously.

I am here in the sun a long time. No one bothers me. My fingers are happy, touching God. And most good of all, my advisor's voice recedes before the pure carnality of sunlight.

Only this morning he admonished me on his single subject.

—I say to men, do not be attracted by the whisper and innuendo of silks, by jewels at the throat, nor by displays of gold bracelets. If you must be near woman, choose one who mourns and fasts, squalid with dirt, almost blind with weeping. No other should interest you but the one who slips to her knees with exhaustion.

—And do men heed you? I asked.

—There are those for whom it is a struggle, he concedes.

—Above all, he concluded, —keep yourself from the sun. For the sun is God's eye. You must not flaunt yourself before Him.

Such flaunting now appears to me attractive. When I have finished my harvesting, I take off the parts of my habit until I am all flesh. I lie down amidst the flax and daisy and let the sun stroke me. This light is like a god with many hands, laying them upon me in every part at once.

I float, my gaze wandering among the clouds. Then, out of the air, Christ appears. Again he resembles an ordinary man, stands in a mist shimmering with rainbow prisms.

—Oh my Lord! I say, and leap up to clothe myself. He discreetly turns away to admire some pansies. When I am dressed, I clear my throat. He turns back to me.

—Catherine, he says. —You shall begin to teach men.

He watches my face to see how I like this.

—The world is filled with wicked men, Catherine. Yet I am determined to bring them right. Into their wickedness you shall speak the Divine Word. When they hear a woman whom they are taught to despise preach and discourse upon scripture, those proud shall be brought low.

—Already I have dropped them several notches, I say.

—But how shall I speak thus? I know not God's knowledge.

—I will give you instant knowledge, not just of God, but of the world. Listen to this, Catherine: earth is not the fixed center of things. The moon circles the earth, and just

so earth—yes, Catherine!—circles the su

is unfixed as well. It is even now hurt

space.

—Indeed?

—Indeed. But I give you this only fo

You must not say this abroad, for they

tried to leak this out through a man, an o

the rack. I would preserve you from this

—My Lord, this is exceedingly rich.

—And this is but the beginning, Ca

have all knowledge, secular and divin

study, but by my infused grace.

—But how is such infusion to be per

—Fear not, Catherine. The method is

—And may I continue reading? I say

—Read, Christ says. —For I gave

you love them and take them inside you

and heart. Read, and also dispense the

you. Let men sit at your feet.

—Very well, I say. —Then you may

as your instrument against them. I shall I

—The two of us, he says, —shall en

There in sunlight, among the ferns,

knowledge enter me in every cell at on

the sun, this infusion is most carnal.

knowledge, its vibratory hum across my

lamp burning oil, and indeed even as I e

with my body, I am at the same time c

eats me with his fiery knowing, so that

thing I am entirely surrendered to him.

Enthralled as I am with examining

forget Christ. But he is used to this t

ments. Thus is he satisfied and departs

of gold bracelets. If you must be near woman, choose one who mourns and fasts, squalid with dirt, almost blind with weeping. No other should interest you but the one who slips to her knees with exhaustion.

—And do men heed you? I asked.

—There are those for whom it is a struggle, he concedes.

—Above all, he concluded, —keep yourself from the sun. For the sun is God's eye. You must not flaunt yourself before Him.

Such flaunting now appears to me attractive. When I have finished my harvesting, I take off the parts of my habit until I am all flesh. I lie down amidst the flax and daisy and let the sun stroke me. This light is like a god with many hands, laying them upon me in every part at once.

I float, my gaze wandering among the clouds. Then, out of the air, Christ appears. Again he resembles an ordinary man, stands in a mist shimmering with rainbow prisms.

—Oh my Lord! I say, and leap up to clothe myself. He discreetly turns away to admire some pansies. When I am dressed, I clear my throat. He turns back to me.

—Catherine, he says. —You shall begin to teach men.

He watches my face to see how I like this.

—The world is filled with wicked men, Catherine. Yet I am determined to bring them right. Into their wickedness you shall speak the Divine Word. When they hear a woman whom they are taught to despise preach and discourse upon scripture, those proud shall be brought low.

—Already I have dropped them several notches, I say.

—But how shall I speak thus? I know not God's knowledge.

—I will give you instant knowledge, not just of God, but of the world. Listen to this, Catherine: earth is not the fixed center of things. The moon circles the earth, and just

STORIES BY MARILYN KRYSL

so earth—yes, Catherine!—circles the sun. And the sun too is unfixed as well. It is even now hurtling through vast space.

—Indeed?

—Indeed. But I give you this only for private perusal. You must not say this abroad, for they will kill you. I have tried to leak this out through a man, and he was put upon the rack. I would preserve you from this.

—My Lord, this is exceedingly rich.

—And this is but the beginning, Catherine. You shall have all knowledge, secular and divine, not by human study, but by my infused grace.

—But how is such infusion to be performed?

—Fear not, Catherine. The method is platonic.

—And may I continue reading? I say.

—Read, Christ says. —For I gave you words because you love them and take them inside you, into your mouth and heart. Read, and also dispense the wisdom I will give you. Let men sit at your feet.

—Very well, I say. —Then you may use my despised sex as your instrument against them. I shall enjoy it.

—The two of us, he says, —shall enjoy it together.

There in sunlight, among the ferns, I feel the body of knowledge enter me in every cell at once. Like the light of the sun, this infusion is most carnal. I feel the heat of knowledge, its vibratory hum across my skin. I glow like a lamp burning oil, and indeed even as I eat God's knowledge with my body, I am at the same time consumed by it. God eats me with his fiery knowing, so that in knowing everything I am entirely surrendered to him.

Enthralled as I am with examining my new condition, I forget Christ. But he is used to this trance in his instruments. Thus is he satisfied and departs.

I announce Christ's infusion to my sisters. Their high, excited voices spread my word. The nunnery is showered with rich gifts, and many young women petition to enter our order. Men of stature, men of wealth, men of standing in the church, government officials, merchants and monastery scribes come to hear me. Though I know no Latin, I explain difficult passages, first reading out the passage in vernacular for the benefit of those who know no Latin, then giving a pithy capsule of it, then elaborating upon that capsule. Except Sunday when I must pray all day, men flock to me. I become every scholar's fetish. For a woman of knowledge is a thing wondrous and monstrous to see.

My advisor is hard put to secure my virginity.

—Tell me again, I say, for he delights to be asked this question. —What is the reason women are better virgin than not?

—It is that those not virgins give birth. Their openings, once unsealed, leak blood and other filthy liquids. Thus it would not be proper that a woman sit in any seat of power. For that would stain and defile the seat for the man who ought properly to sit there.

—But a virgin, though she too bleeds filthy liquids, might sit there?

—No no, he replies. —I shall explain. A virgin is the best there is of this evil. For the womb itself is a place of destruction.

—Did you say, sir, a palace of delectation?

—Listen well, he replies. —The womb is unclean.

—Indeed it is unseen and unmean.

—Have you lost your hearing? It is a dirty fountain!

—Certainly, sir. A pretty mountain indeed.

—You seem to refuse my instruction, he says.

—Oh no sir, I say, casting my eyes down, then once again gazing at him.   I but give you opportunity to instruct. I then echo your instruction as best I can.

My guest descends from heaven with cooling balm in a green pitcher. I delight in her company, and we love to whisper gossip. We lie on my cot, the length of us touching. Around us, dark is the velvet water of the womb.

—The fathers believe no clitoris is to be found on a virtuous woman, my guest whispers. —For once a witch hunter, examining a woman, found one on her, and he had never seen such a thing. He thought it resembled a Devil's teat, and brought other men to see it. They too had never seen such a growth, and agreed it was proof against her.

—They had never seen a woman's nether parts at all, I say. —For my advisor has told me the married do not undress. Rather, the woman sews a slit in her gown so her husband may enter without touching her.

—Catherine, know this: in the Greek language, *clitoris* means divine.

—May Greeks who are so wise have long life, I say.

—While you praise them, she says —I shall enjoy your divinity.

She touches me on that hot little pouch, and there comes to be much shimmering in me. It is indeed just as Christ said: I can feel the sun hurtling through space.

However, on this night, after my guest leaves, there is rustling in the hall. Then silence. I light my candle, tiptoe to the door, open it a crack. Then farther. Someone has left at my door a chamber pot piled high with feces. The smell is a rich insult, and I go immediately to empty it, lest the rest of the night be soiled with its odor. So, I think, I have been admonished for my tartness. Or is it for my smartness? Perhaps both.

I am called to Rome to expound upon scripture. Though the Pope must be away in Germany, his minions will examine me in his name. I am thrilled at this news. Then I wonder: is it possible this wish to examine me is fueled by the Pope's hope that I shall fail? I should like to consult Christ on this matter. But when I cast about for some means by which to summon him, it is my advisor who appears.

—I say to men this, he begins. —There is a danger for you in one whose face you are continually watching. Rip yourself from this looking. Above all, do not linger on the shape of a woman's body which you imagine beneath her cloak. Tear your vision from her and walk on quickly. For watching is itself an enchantment, and the watching of prettiness is temptation laid by devilish women. And know this: anything that is shaped like the body will distract you. Even a simple flower may suggest lewdness. My advice to men is to keep your gaze busy, to turn your eyes continuously away to some other object.

—Your eyes are most piercing blue, I say.

He does not reply.

This same afternoon I gather Galega for the sisters, and enough more to brew a bath for my guest's feet. When I have finished this task, I cut bunches of Chaste Tree, enough to fill two baskets. I go to my advisor's room, bustle in, spread the Chaste Tree stems on his mattress, laying them down with great spectacle and flourish.

—This, sir, is to bring you restful sleep.

—Indeed? And what is this herb?

—This is Chaste Tree, I say. —The blossoms and leaves of Chaste Tree subdue lust, which to men is troublesome.

My guest comes in a cerulean robe, velvet thick as a moonless evening's dark. But the belt of her garment is a cord that wraps around her more than thrice. There is much unwinding to get it off her.

—Why so much precaution? I tease.

—There is good reason. For if ever I must leave the convent, I shall slide down the outer wall on this leverage.

—I beg you, do not go. Instead I shall bind you with this cord to keep you near me.

—You need not. For I am kept at your bosom already by the leash of your beauty.

She kisses my throat. —Now let the fire rage, she whispers. —For fire burns itself out. Then you shall be calm.

She lies beside me and stokes the flame until it rises in conflagration. When I begin to cry out, she lightly lays her palm across my mouth, lest I wake the sleeping sisters.

My advisor travels with me to guard my virginity. But in truth I think he likes to be seen with me, since he has no importance of his own.

—Sir, I say, as the carriage rolls, I wonder, is it not suggestive that a fully formed man like yourself be seen traveling alone with a virgin?

—I travel with you in my capacity as learned teacher. All recognize the wisdom of a virgin girl needing accompaniment. There are brigands on the roads from whom, should need arise, I shall defend your honor. And we may use the time to increase your understanding of the dangers your sex broadcasts.

—But sir, might you yourself not be tempted, as a man and weak-fleshed? For you are indeed a man, are you not? And are you not weak-fleshed?

—Certainly I am man. But I am not weak. Though it may tax me, I practice abstinence. I have made no motion toward you through all our lessons.

—Indeed, sir. Not a single motion, only to look me in the eye as you speak.

—A teacher cannot avoid looking at his pupil. Thus are we teachers the more virtuous, for we are ever being sorely tested.

—Indeed, sir, you are to be commended, I say, or some such blather to match his own.

We put up along the way at a convent. The sisters are happy to see me, and I eat as much as I like. Afterward my advisor comes to weigh me on a scale he has purchased for this purpose.

—You have gained severally, he says, in dismay. —You had best get back to a good long fast, lest you slip away from Christ's hope for you.

—Christ's hope for me is that I do his work in the world. Therefore I must have sustenance.

—He would not wish it at risk of your overindulgence.

—Then I pray you, sir, assist me in Christ's work by taking on this stringent fasting for me. Christ will admire your generous act, and you may transfer the credits to me.

Near the Vatican we get down, go on foot to the cathedral. I am flanked on both sides by eager scholars, and before me, at my bosom, like a crier, strides my advisor. I do not keep my eyes to the pavement in modesty. Rather I survey the faces of these Romans, the architecture of their shops and living quarters. I am busy with the smell of spices, the music of a wandering band of singers. In a narrow lane approaching the cathedral, a clot of men advances toward us. They come on like a company of soldiers.

—Let us see this witch! one cries.

My advisor clears his throat, and calls out.

—Stand away from this holy virgin! This charge of mine whom I have tutored from childhood, and who has learned much at my feet, will pass into the cathedral to deliver up the wisdom I have given her.

—She is no virgin who expounds like a man, says one.

—Let us find out her chastity, says another. —Show us thy opening, wench!

My scholars are aghast. The language of the street is too raw for their prim ears. A crowd now surrounds us. My advisor dances, miming acts of defense, but he can do no more than bristle. The men surge forward and they spit at me. My scholars wince and hop back. Most spittle falls at my feet, but some arrives upon my cloak. The crowd sends up exclamation. Voices cry out in protest. Some in the crowd fall to scuffling in my defense. Amidst much shouting, the spitters are forced to disband.

My advisor turns to me, a little smile upon his mouth.

—They have spit upon you, he says. —You have suffered defilement.

I lean and whisper so that only he may hear.

—Get down on your knees then, and lick it up.

The cathedral ceiling seems so high as to be the sky itself, painted with billows of cloud and angels gliding. The altar is set with chalices, the high walls hung with tapestries, the carpets over the stone aisles woven in Cathay. I mount to the high seat and begin. I float in my body a little upward. For I come to know wisdom even at the moment I speak it, and this coming to know is like filling with a sweet froth. I am listening and learning, as are the others. But it is myself I learn from.

My face is neither exceptionally beautiful, nor is it flawed. And my habit covers me so that no one can surmise the lineaments of my body. But the ravenous minds of these lookers are busy picturing me naked. For surely, they think, the body of one who speaks thusly must be either of great ugliness or great beauty. They are baffled as to which it can be.

A man questions me in haughty tones. I answer simply but with insight, quoting from the works of the gospels, the holy writings of saints. Afterward this man can say nothing. Another questions. My words enter him, and he is deprived of speech. It is as Christ predicted: men are cast low by my knowledge. After a while no one ventures to stand before me. I rise and declare our audience at an end.

The crowd files out after me in silence. No more can they bang their chests with proud fists. And when they return home, their wives will wonder at their shrinking and loss of appetite. Though before they leave Rome, they will seek remedy, some in the dark arms of wine and liquor, but most to the brothel. There they may manage to revive themselves somewhat by their own so-called filthy coitus, carried out in leashed anger as a punishment of me upon the woman at hand.

If they can get their bodies to obey their little minds.

If in fact they can forget me.

My advisor has taken ill. He must give up his rich breakfast, and is able to enter the carriage only with difficulty.
Our travel is hindered by much stopping of the horses,
for he must get down to retch in the ditch. Afterward he
reenters the carriage only with the help of the footman.

I bathe his forehead with my handkerchief. —You will
be better soon, I say.

He groans. Speech for once has fled his tongue, and I wonder: perhaps the words could bear no more his usage of them.

Thus I am free of his instruction. We ride through the
countryside in blessed silence. I enjoy the scenery, send
loving remembrance to my father, and gaze ahead, savoring
what Christ shows me the future will bring: the differential
calculus, a machine which moves by power of the air that
rises from a pot of boiling broth. Invisible force made to
flow through strands of metal which produces light in the
midst of darkness. And a powerful spectacle for one eye
through which men will see the various parts our blood is
made of, even the tiniest particles of our beings.

We arrive into chaos. In my absence the nunnery has come
under siege from the archbishop. Though I was called to
Rome by the Pope, though I left with the Mother's bless-
ing, the archbishop has sent his man to chastise her for
allowing my travel without seeking his permission through
proper channels. She delivers this news. Then she smiles.

—Many came out to see you in Rome, she says. —We
have heard with proud excitement of your fame.

—Yes, Mother. But I fear the crowds in that great city
were of such numbers that the archbishop has been cast in
shadow.

The Mother covers her giggling with a plump hand.

—Indeed, she says. —Thus we must devise some penance for you to satisfy him. Her eyes twinkle. —What shall it be?

—Since I have been too much in the world, you may confine me to my cell for a sequence of nights, I say. —And since I am known to love fasting, send some mutton and rampion with dumplings, followed by honey cakes. I shall be forced to swallow these for my sins.

—This is fit penance, she says. —And during the day, for full measure, I shall censure you to wander long hours in the woods where you shall be exposed to the noxious perfume of flowers and the noisome cackling of birds.

My guest comes in darkness with a basket of wild irises. She brings mead made by her own hand. She brings bread and sausage and milk and sundry fruits, and a cake made of sugar and walnuts.

—I cannot eat more, I say. —For the Mother is feeding me as a penance. You eat and I will watch. Now hear what I have decided. I shall insist on another trip to Rome, now that my advisor is ill. Thus shall I request your presence as a substitute for his.

—It is a pretty plan, my guest whispers. —And if I may not go in your advisor's place, perhaps I may go as your handmaiden. You know how wondrous are my hands in your service.

—I shall testify to your credentials for this work, I whisper. —Further, I shall demonstrate where and how you gave me your ministrations, here, and here, and here.

—We must not laugh more, she whispers. —I must kiss your mouth to stop your chattering.

—Not my mouth only, I pray you. I have other lips which want your kissing.

Next morning the stinking chamber pot is once again at my door. How its bearer must have struggled to perform this deposit!

After breakfast I am called to my advisor's chamber. He would instruct me there, but he has not yet recovered from his fever. I confess I take advantage of his weakness to advise him.

—Be not overly proud, I say. —For pretension is the Devil's work. It is unbecoming in a man to strut and preen, or to expound at too great length on subjects of which he knows but little. For though pride may seem a shiny thing, in truth it contains foul smelling murk and stink, the odor of which assaults Christ's nostrils.

—This illness is for your good instruction, I say. —It will subdue unseemly pride and the fever inspire you to ardent fasting. Remember what you yourself have counseled: that to fast will deliver you directly up to God. Persevere. You shall inspire us all.

When the sun sits low, I gather Shepherd's Purse and Wallflower for my advisor. Wallflower purifies the blood, and Shepherd's Purse will staunch internal bleeding. For I have bethought myself: my thrusts upon a sick man were unkind. Nor do I want to resemble him in my actions. I resolve that when I have gathered these herbs, I shall take them to him, along with a cup of broth, a piece of bread, and a tiny cherry tart, that he not expire on my account.

I also gather Passion Flower for myself, this plant which has in its body Christ's story. The flower's crown is his crown of thorns. The stamens are his wounds, the ovary the sponge soaked in vinegar. The three styles represent three nails, and the five sepals and five petals the ten apostles, leaving out Peter who denied Christ and Judas who betrayed him. My gathering of Passion Flower is spiritual labor. By it I honor Christ who has brought me equally into his company. I like to think of him, the only man besides my father I can imagine loving.

When I go to my advisor, he struggles to sit up.

—I must instruct you, he says. —Do not wash yourself in the presence of the other sisters. When you bathe, take care that your own hand not touch you but only the cloth. Keep yourself pure, and retire to your cell early and pray. I fear for your soul, if you are too much in the world.

Great sweat is everywhere on him from his effort.

—You will be better soon, I say. —Advise me then.

—I am advising you now, he says through tightly held teeth.

That evening my guest brings vegetable morsels, hearty bread, a pot of pudding. The night sky is black as the fur of a bear. The gibbous moon floats, a heaped boat.

—I am forbidden to touch myself, I say. —You must do it.

—I shall be pleased to do for you what you cannot do for yourself, she replies.

We laugh and must cover our mouths with the comforter. So we are busy whispering and do not hear the creak in the hall. For surely there must have been creaking. When the moon has fallen to the rim of the hill, I am spent, and my sleepy guest unwinds from me. I watch her pull on her blue robe. Then she kisses my elbow, goes to the door, turns the knob. She turns the knob again, with force.

She comes back to the cot and kneels at my side.

—Catherine, she says. —We are found out.

3

My father pleads to visit me in prison. The church authorities agree he may come one time only. When he comes,
holding his hat with both hands, my eyes will not give up
his face. The anguish upon him is like a painting, so rich I
must have more leisure in which to discover its gifts.

—Father, I say. —I am very lonely, and in my loneliness
you have come to me.

—Catherine, I fail you. For I have pleaded every way for
your liberty, but I cannot make them say yes to it.

—The Mother too has tried, but she cannot. Many others petitioned the archbishop on my behalf. But my fame
has grown too broad. The archbishop will not let me go,
even if Christ were to demand it.

My father's jaw quivers. —How will you bear their
questioning?

—We shall see, I say. —But quickly now, I must question you. I must know this: how did my mother die?

He looks at me a long moment. —I cannot tell you.

—You must. For I am going to die.

My father lowers his face into his hands. When he lets
his hands drop, his face is a ravaged thing no woman would
want to be the cause of.

—Just as your friend's mother was questioned, just so,
many years before, they took your mother. You were but a
baby, and I was forced quickly to find you a wet nurse. I
was in agony with anxiousness, and went every day where
they kept your mother. She denied their charges, but they
told me she was haughty and thus very likely guilty. Have
you not noticed her ways? they said. I said I had not. But
they did not heed me.

—There was a test they liked to use then, the test of a
very large cauldron of water. If the woman drowned, that

would prove her magic devil's tricks and her guilt. If she could find a way out, that would prove her innocence. But in truth, Catherine, the cauldron was deep, and the sides high and slippery.

A cry rips from my throat. My father takes both of my hands in his.

—Afterward, my father says, they bade me come and take away her body. At that same time they bade me bring you to them. I lied and said I would bring you at once. Instead, I escaped with you and the wet nurse. Many days we traveled through several countries to this place. Here there had been no questioning of women. Here I thought you would be safe.

I lay my head in my father's lap. He bends above me, kisses my shaved head. I think back to that swell of breast, which seemed to hold me within its circumference, and from which I drew forth my first food.

—So the breast I remember was very likely not my mother's?

—Very likely not, my father says. —And now you know all Christ tells you, and this, which he did not.

I have been granted permission to visit my advisor this last time. Guards in black hoods take me in the dark to a covered carriage. For the archbishop fears that the populace, should it become known who rides within, might bar passage and take me out to save me from destruction. These guards escort me to my advisor's chamber. They go out, one to watch the door, the other the window. I am alone with my man. He lies on his sheet, wet with fever. His head turns to one side, then, after some moments, to the other.

I take his hand, thinking perhaps the touch of a virgin may startle him into health. But he does not sit up exclaiming

that he has been defiled. He is all the way below me now, as
he never dreamed he would be.

—Sir, I say. —I have come to speak to you one to
another. I pray not that you forgive my sauciness, for I do
not consider it a sin. My prayer is that you take me into
your heart as I am, a woman whose voice resounds through
cathedrals, a woman who delights in the lascivious dark.

His breath is labored, his eyes closed. I do not think he
has heard me. Still, I am better for having spoken. I who had
despised him now examine myself: I do not wish him any ill.

Nor is death an illness. In life's great turning it is but one
small bit of the turn. I wonder if he knows this. I lean and
put my lips close to his ear.

—Sir, I say, —where you go we all are going. Know you
do not go alone.

Her name was Beatrice. By this name I called her many
times. She was quick witted and moxie sweet, and there
was a small mole above her left breast which I liked to kiss,
and a scar on her ankle.

I used to gather rhizomes of the male fern. A good supply
of these I had hidden in my cell against emergency. But immediately they separated us, and took the rhizomes before I
could swallow them. Beatrice begged to be sent to her cell, so
that she might recover a handkerchief she had of her mother.
They shrugged and let her go, only guarding the door and
window. There she threw the cord from her cerulean robe
over the rafter, tied a noose, climbed inside it and swung.

Now I eat God in the dark, since I may not nibble the
mouth of Beatrice. I wonder if Christ will come to me again.

I am most grateful that he gave me reading, though I have begun to think there is much written that is not worth the page on which it is inscribed. I love the power of reciting holy texts aloud, but these books offer up much nonsense, and they repeat and repeat in the manner of my advisor. A few kind travelers have slipped me a book of theirs, and thus have I read some philosophers. But they go on at tedious length, though they know little of life.

I know the world as it is with us, passing through us in trembling waves. So I think, and so I thought, all those days I gathered Star Thistle to sell in the market. Herbs bring in money for our convent, for people are ever seeking remedies for the body. They would preserve even their finger-nails. They fear the end of their fearful lives.

But fear is the great shrinker. It eats away at the liver. It terrorizes the nerves. And they are so distracted by its harrying, that they cannot enjoy the little feasts that are served to us each moment.

If Christ comes or does not, it shall not matter. I shall have had my million moments. The cool earth will be a calm place to sleep, and I will be among the good grains of the soil. In the meantime I eat God as He eats me, both of us gaining as we lose.

Christ's wounded body comes to me in a dream. He has been unnailed and taken down by his disciples, and they have laid him on a slab of stone in moonlight. I approach and examine his palms and feet. The bloody holes are there, and the wound in his side. I kneel beside him, take his hurt hand in mine. I kiss the palm, then bend across him. The gash left by the soldier's spear is half rip, half puncture. I lean and lay my lips on his wound.

This kiss onto his suffering gives me great swelling love. I am ocean throwing itself against the sand shore. Then I must draw back, for I notice, at the corner of my eye, a fleshy stalk. Christ's member, just near my cheek, has risen like a standard. It is fully stretched to its upper limit. And now, behold, it speaks.

—Catherine, it calls. —I am a little dead man, so I can do you no harm. Now give me your kiss. Your kissing is very pretty. Come kiss me on the very top of my head.

I fly awake, as though hurled out through layers of shutters and more shutters. This one time I need not muffle my laughter. And I think of the archbishop, in his chamber, hiding in his heart his human longing for a lover. For surely he longs. He is flesh, and like us comes down with the influenza. If I could, I would give him my dream. He might put it to better use than I.